RODNEY STRONG

Antiques and Assault

© Copyright 2022 Rodney Strong

Rodney Strong asserts his moral right to be identified as the author of this work.

ISBN: 978-1-991155-62-7

All rights reserved. No part of this publication may be produced or transmitted in any form or by any means, electronic or mechanical, including photocopying, recording or information storage and retrieval systems, without permission in writing from the copyright holder.

Published by LoreQuinn Publishing

This is a work of fiction. Names, characters, places, and incidents either are the production of the author's imagination or are used fictitiously, and any resemblance to actual persons, living or dead, events, or locales is entirely coincidental.

Editor: Anna Golden

Front cover design: www.stunningbookcovers.com

A catalogue record for this book is available from the National Library of New Zealand.

This book was professionally typeset on Reedsy.
Find out more at reedsy.com

Contents

Chapter 1	1
ONE	2
TWO	6
THREE	13
FOUR	17
FIVE	24
SIX	28
SEVEN	35
EIGHT	41
NINE	49
TEN	55
ELEVEN	63
TWELVE	69
THIRTEEN	76
FOURTEEN	84
FIFTEEN	92
SIXTEEN	98
SEVENTEEN	107
EIGHTEEN	113
NINETEEN	125
TWENTY	132
TWENTY-ONE	140
TWENTY-TWO	149
TWENTY-THREE	159

TWENTY-FOUR	164
TWENTY-FIVE	173
TWENTY-SIX	180
TWENTY-SEVEN	189
TWENTY-EIGHT	194
TWENTY-NINE	202
THIRTY	209
THIRTY-ONE	217
THIRTY-TWO	222
THIRTY-THREE	225
THIRTY-FOUR	229
THIRTY-FIVE	233
About the Author	237
Also by Rodney Strong	238

Chapter 1

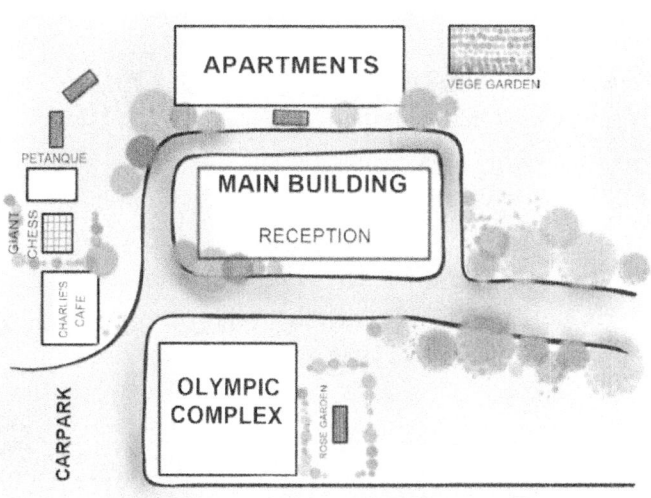

ONE

Wellington, March 1994

'Why can't we have a fancier house?'

'Because fancy houses are for people that have things worth stealing.'

'But we have things worth stealing.'

'Yes, but we don't want them stolen.'

Amanda glared at her grandmother.

Alice liked to say she'd lasted through a world war, the death of the only man she'd loved, the death of her daughter, and the odd attempt on her own life, but dealing with a twelve-year-old was more challenging than them all.

'We can talk about this later,' said Alice.

'But Grandma …'

Alice winced. 'Don't call me that.'

Amanda grinned. While the name was technically correct, the reminder that she was old enough to be a grandmother got on Alice's nerves – which was precisely why Amanda did it.

'Alright, then. *Alice*. Why can't we move to a nicer house?'

ONE

'I said we'll talk about it later. Focus on your task.'

Amanda held up the open padlock. 'Done.'

Alice approved. Although lockpicking wasn't typically part of a pre-teen's curriculum, it was an essential skill in Alice's view.

She wasn't teaching Amanda so she could go into the same line of work as her own, however. She'd made that clear. But you never knew when you might get locked out – of your house or someone else's.

'Nice work.' Alice plucked the lockpick out of Amanda's right hand and handed her another padlock.

'Do it again.'

'But you took my lockpick.'

'Improvise.'

Amanda looked at Alice uncertainly, then her face set in a determined expression and she scanned the room.

'Who is Helen Gregory?' asked Alice.

Amanda mumbled a reply.

'So my tired old ears can hear, dear.'

Amanda rolled her eyes but stepped out of reach first. 'Just a girl at school.'

'And?'

'And nothing. She's annoying and stuck up and a total waste of oxygen.'

Alice waited.

Amanda sighed and continued. 'She told everyone my mum was dead.'

'Your mother is dead.'

'I know that!' Amanda shot her a look. 'But she's going around school calling me "the orphan".'

'You are an—'

'Don't.'

'Amanda, my dear, there will always be people in this world that will say bad things to you or about you. Some think it's clever, some are deflecting attention from the problems in their own lives, and some are simply stupid. But you must decide whether they are going to upset you.'

A tear escaped from Amanda's eye. She angrily wiped it away and kept examining the padlock. She reached out and plucked the brooch from Alice's blouse. Bending the pin, she set to work on the lock.

Alice said. 'An orphan means you no longer have a living mother or father. It doesn't mean you have no family. It doesn't mean you aren't loved.'

She regretted it the moment the words came out of her mouth.

Amanda smiled. 'You love me?'

'Finish your task.'

'You said you loved me.'

'Such a shame they got rid of workhouses in New Zealand.'

Amanda paused. 'How did you know about Helen?'

'You wrote *I hate Helen Gregory* on your notebook. Front page. Very disappointing.'

'But I do.'

'What did I say about people with fancy houses?'

Amanda frowned at the sudden change in topic. 'That we can't have one?'

'That they advertise that they have things worth stealing. Writing that you hate Helen Gregory on the front of your notebook, where Helen and anyone else can see it, is letting her know that she's getting to you. You're giving her the advantage.'

'So I should hide my feelings? Didn't you always tell me

ONE

not to push my feelings down so deep they became blocks of concrete around my ankles?'

Alice winced. 'Something to that effect. I'm not saying you should let Helen get away with anything. You have a right to be upset. But there are better ways.'

There was a faint click and Amanda held up the open padlock and the bent brooch. 'Sorry about your brooch, Gran.'

'*Gran*,' Alice repeated with a scowl.

'Worse?'

'Much.'

TWO

Wellington, August 2021

'Do you remember Helen Gregory?'

Alice blinked and rifled through her memory. The name rang a bell but she couldn't place it. She shook her head at her granddaughter.

'I was twelve. She was my arch enemy for about two weeks.'

'Oh, the blonde girl with the big mouth and bigger attitude. Arch enemy is probably overselling it a bit. What about her?'

Amanda (also blonde, but without the big mouth and high opinion of herself) stood up and smoothed her pants. She crossed to the kitchen and poured two cups of tea from the pot brewing on the counter.

It was a dark day outside. Dull sunlight battled clouds and tinted glass to provide natural light in the large penthouse apartment and Amanda paused to switch on the lights before carrying the two cups back.

'I ran into her today. She had no idea who I was of course. I was very restrained.'

TWO

'Who did she think you were?'

'I can't remember. I just made up a name on the spot. Joyce something.'

'Joyce Kendrick?'

Amanda looked at Alice in surprise. 'Yes, I think it was. How on Earth did you know that?'

'Joyce Kendrick was your first teacher at primary school.'

'Really? I'd completely forgotten.'

'Amanda, you have to be more careful,' Alice admonished her. 'Why did you lie anyway?'

'She sort of recognised me so I had to come up with something. I'm not totally silly. You know full well I couldn't tell her who I was. Not after what happened at school. Or have you forgotten?'

Alice had forgotten until just now. She smiled down into her teacup. That had been a fun learning experience for Amanda.

'Anyway, that wasn't my news. When I was talking to Helen, she let slip that her grandmother was moving into Silvermoon.'

Alice frowned. 'I hadn't heard that.'

'And I thought you knew everything around here.'

'There is a fine line between being knowledgeable and nosy.'

Before Amanda could respond, the apartment door opened and a young woman entered carrying two shopping bags.

'Hey guys.'

'A hundred years of fighting for equality and we still get "hello guys",' Alice said sourly.

'You're not quite at a hundred yet,' Amanda replied with a grin.

'I meant women in general. One more quip like that and you're out of my will.'

Amanda didn't appear bothered. She'd made it clear many

times over the years that the only thing she wanted from Alice was for the old woman to live forever.

'Sorry, *Gran*.'

Alice turned up her nose in disgust.

Amanda laughed. 'Is shopping part of your training?' she asked Vanessa.

Until recently Vanessa Carson had worked as a receptionist at the Silvermoon Retirement Village. Now she worked directly for Alice in a capacity that was proving hard to explain to her friends and family. She wasn't a companion exactly, although she liked Alice's company. And she couldn't tell her mother that Alice was teaching her skills that might be employed in less than legal circumstances. So she kept descriptions of her work vague.

'Apparently. But I draw the line at cleaning,' Vanessa replied with a grin. She absently retied her long brown hair into a ponytail and unloaded the bags of food into the fridge. At twenty-four, she moved with the casual ease that Alice vaguely remembered from her own youth.

Alice turned back to her granddaughter. 'So what if Helen Gregory's grandmother is moving in? Why does that deserve a headline?'

Amanda shrugged. 'Didn't you teach me that knowledge is power? I didn't want you to be surprised.'

Alice nodded approvingly. 'When is she arriving?'

'Today. In fact …' Amanda went to the large window overlooking the front of the retirement village. 'I believe that's her moving truck.'

Alice struggled to her feet, stood for a moment to steady herself, then carefully walked her ninety-eight-year-old body over to the window. Her right ankle, injured months ago, took

TWO

a few steps to warm up. She refused to use the walking stick propped next to her bed.

Two floors below, a man leant against a mid-sized white removal truck. They watched him pull something from his pocket and place it to his mouth. A puff of smoke came out. Then he put the object back in his pocket.

'That is not a sensible thing to do with a lit cigarette,' Alice said.

'It's a vape.'

'A what?'

'It simulates smoking without actually smoking,' Amanda explained.

'What's the point?' muttered Alice.

A second man came down the front steps and pointed to the inner part of the complex.

'What are you two looking at? Oh, that must be Mrs Gregory's stuff.'

'Why must it be?' Alice demanded.

'Gary and Sherry Iverson moved out last week. There's only one empty apartment in the village.'

Alice hadn't known the Iversons beyond a casual nod in passing. She had a small group of friends at Silvermoon and suffered no great desire for more. There were sixty residents at the Silvermoon Retirement Village, none as old as Alice, and none with her unique background. Those not counted as friends (or marked as potential rivals) were mostly dismissed from Alice's thoughts.

'What do you know about her?'

Vanessa shrugged. 'Not a lot. I don't keep track of all the comings and goings anymore.'

Amanda winced.

Alice scowled. 'Knowledge is power, Vanessa. Nothing is too trivial.'

'Then why don't you know?' Vanessa replied.

'Because I have you.'

'I swear I've had this same conversation with my Mum,'

There was a knock at the front door. Out of habit Alice reached for her phone to check the security camera. Cameras weren't standard at Silvermoon, but Alice had had one installed when she moved in. She liked security cameras. Now if Alice was alone or simply wanted to avoid talking to someone, she could check the app on her phone to see who was there and decide not to answer it.

'I'll get it,' Vanessa said.

She crossed to the door and opened it a fraction, letting her body fill the gap, Alice nodded approvingly. The way she was standing prevented the visitor seeing too much of the apartment and, most importantly, allowed Vanessa to lie about Alice's availability.

'Hi, Owen.'

Vanessa stepped aside and Alice smiled warmly as Owen strode into the room. Long retired, the tall distinguished ex-bank executive still wore a shirt and tie every day and aside from the grey hair and wrinkled face, looked as if he could just as easily have been walking into a boardroom.

'Ladies,' he said as a greeting.

'How's Rachel?' Alice asked. She waved him into a seat on the couch, then settled herself back into her armchair.

'She's doing fine. Loving university.'

Alice had helped his granddaughter out of a tight spot earlier in the year.

'She says she'll visit at the end of the semester. I'll make sure

TWO

she comes to say hello.'

'Good. Now what brings you here today. We didn't have an appointment, did we?'

'No,' Owen replied with a reassuring smile. Then the smile dropped from his face and he played with his cufflinks.

'What is it, Owen?'

He sighed. 'I've got myself into a bit of bother.'

Alice perked up. She'd become a solver of problems for her friends. Far from minding, she appreciated the chance to dust off her old skills and exercise her brain. She leaned in. 'Tell me.'

'I've been asked to give a speech.'

Alice blinked. 'Is that it? Surely you've given hundreds of them over the years.'

'Yes, but they were all business-related and in person. This one is …' He breathed heavily, looking much older than his seventy-nine years. 'I've been asked to give a speech *online*.'

He paused to let the horror of that statement sink in.

'*Online*,' he repeated.

Amanda came to sit down on the couch beside him. 'Don't worry, Owen. Vanessa can help you set it up.'

'Sure, easy as.'

Owen relaxed into his chair. 'Thank you, dear. I would hate to press the wrong button and cut everyone off.'

'What's your speech about?' asked Alice.

Before he could answer, a loud crash came from outside. Amanda and Vanessa rushed to the window, followed by the two retirees at a more leisurely pace. Below, the truck was still in the same spot and a large wooden crate lay on the ground at the back of the truck. The two workers were fighting beside it.

'How unprofessional,' Owen said primly.

'My money's on the big guy,' Vanessa said.

'Vanessa!'

'Sorry.'

'I should think so. The other man is clearly going to win.'

Before either could be proven right, a woman came rushing down the front steps. Although they couldn't hear what she was saying, the men immediately stopped fighting and looked down at their feet.

'Go Tracey,' Alice murmured.

Tracey Miller was Manager of the Silvermoon Retirement Village. Alice typically found the woman too officious for her liking. She was ideally suited to running a place the size of Silvermoon, but not for someone to have a satisfying conversation with.

In no time at all the men had picked up the box and placed it in the back of the truck. The men closed the truck door and one of them shook Tracey's hand while the other brushed past her on his way to the cab.

The others turned away from the window, but Alice stayed watching a moment longer.

'Now that's...'

THREE

Wellington, March 1994

'… interesting,' Alice said.

Amanda slumped in her seat and avoided eye contact with either adult.

'Interesting is not the word I would use, Mrs Strong. Your granddaughter was caught stealing from another student's bag.'

Amanda snuck a sideways look at her grandmother. Amanda knew she never trusted someone who insisted on using a formal title after you'd generously given permission for them to address you by your first name.

Alice was gazing the officious-looking woman on the other side of the desk with a steely eye. 'I doubt that, Frances.'

Principal Frances Kingston was in her fifties, married with two children, and had been a school principal for five years. She hadn't volunteered any of this information, but between the framed pictures on the desk, and diplomas on the wall it wasn't hard for Amanda to build a picture.

'I can assure you—'

'Did anyone see her in the other girl's bag?'

The principal looked flustered at being interrupted. 'Well, no, but items from the student's bag were found in Amanda's desk and the student—'

'Helen.'

'Excuse me?'

'She's made a serious allegation against my granddaughter. She doesn't get to hide behind the moniker of *student*. There's no anonymity here. Items from Helen Gregory's bag were found in Amanda's desk. Is that correct?'

'Er, well, yes.'

Alice shifted in her seat and silently cursed hard wooden chairs. 'Does my granddaughter seem stupid to you?'

Frances Kingston's cheeks darkened and she fiddled with the file of papers on her desk. 'No, she does not. In fact, several of her teachers commented in her last report card that she could do a lot better at school if she applied herself more.'

'So, she's a smart child,' Alice prompted.

'Yes, I believe so.'

'Yet you allege that my smart granddaughter snuck into Helen Gregory's bag, stole some things, and then cleverly hid them in her own desk?'

'Perhaps she didn't have time to dispose of them.'

Alice didn't bother responding to that ridiculous statement.

'Regardless of how it occurred, Helen's silver hairbrush and wallet were found in Amanda's desk.'

'I have no doubt they were,' replied Alice. 'But ask yourself, Frances, do you think it more likely that my brilliant young granddaughter suddenly turned stupid and hid stolen items in the one place someone would look for them? Or is it possible

THREE

that the girl she has been in a dispute with placed them there herself? Tell me, who was it that suggested you look in my granddaughter's desk?'

Frances didn't answer, but a flicker in her eyes told Amanda everything she needed to know.

'You didn't think it suspicious that Helen pointed at Amanda's desk and low and behold that's where the stolen items were found?' Alice said.

Frances shifted in her chair and plucked an invisible piece of lint off her sleeve. 'The animosity between the two girls was brought to my attention. It seemed natural to investigate the most likely culprit first. I was looking for horses, not zebras, Mrs Strong.'

Alice stood up and gestured for Amanda to do the same. 'It seems to me that you'd get to the real culprit a lot faster if you looked for people, not animals. We are done here. There will be no further action taken against my granddaughter or I will take the matter up with the school board. Are we clear?'

Frances slowly got to her feet and escorted them to the door. 'Of course. Thank you for coming down.'

In the hallway Alice remained quiet until they were away from the office area.

'Tell me you didn't take those things,' she murmured.

'Of course I didn't,' Amanda whispered back. 'The first lesson – we're not thieves.'

Alice nodded. 'Then we are faced with two possibilities. Either Helen put them there herself in a clichéd attempt to frame you, or…'

'Or what?'

'Or someone else knew about your dispute and took advantage of it. Which makes me think I didn't ask one important

Antiques and Assault

...'

FOUR

Wellington, August 2021

'...question.'

Alice waited until Owen left before instructing Vanessa to find out everything she could about the woman moving in and more specifically about the moving company.

'I can't be sure they took anything. The angle was wrong and it was quick and ...'

'Your eyes are old.'

'Out.' Alice scowled and pointed to the door. 'And don't come back until you've learnt something useful.'

'Yes, boss,' Vanessa replied with a hint of a salute.

Alice's scowl deepened but Vanessa wisely left quickly.

'Do you want me to stay?' asked Amanda.

'Don't you have work to do?'

Amanda offered her grandmother her arm and Alice reluctantly took it. They walked slowly over to the armchair and Alice settled herself. The ankle injury, which had been self-inflicted in a futile effort to show she wasn't as old as she appeared, still twinged and ached if she stood for too long. The whole thing made her irritable.

'I'm in early planning.'

'Tell me.'

'I will, eventually.'

'I can help.'

Amanda smiled at her. 'Alice, if and when I need your help, I will ask you for it. But you taught me well, and I've been doing this for a while now.'

'Do you ever regret it?'

Amanda sat on the end of the couch closest to Alice. 'Regret what?'

Alice sighed. 'The way I raised you. The life I forced you into.'

Amanda took her hand. 'First, you didn't force me into anything. As if you could. Second, this melancholic reflection is for boring people and you Alice are most definitely not boring.'

'Charming.'

'And third, I love my life. Love it. Wouldn't change it for the world. Understand?'

Alice nodded. She was ashamed of her own weakness. She liked to think she was made of granite. Idle displays of emotion had never been her thing.

Amanda leaned over and kissed her on the cheek. 'I'll call soon. If your nothing with the delivery men turns into a something, you know where to find me.'

By this she meant that Alice knew how to get hold of her. Even a global pandemic hadn't prevented Amanda from flying to other parts of the world and Alice rarely knew exactly where Amanda was. Alice had missed the last worldwide pandemic,

FOUR

which had occurred a couple of years before she was born. As she rarely left Silvermoon these days, she hadn't paid much attention to the current goings on. The only impact it had made to her day-to-day life was that visitors tended to wear masks when coming to and from the complex. It just made them that much harder to keep track of.

After Amanda left, Alice sat and stared out the window. From her chair, she could see the sky and that was about it. Standing at the window, she would have been able to see down the hill to the city below, and the harbour beyond that. It was one of the reasons she had taken this apartment. She wasn't a natural scenery gazer, but it was nice to know she could see what was approaching if she was so inclined.

A restless feeling came over her and she decided to take a short walk outside. She buttoned up a sweater and pulled a woollen hat over her closely cropped grey hair. Then she took the hat off again. It made her look too elderly.

Closing her front door, she crossed the small hallway to the elevator. Hers was one of two apartments on the top floor. Actually that wasn't quite true – though virtually no one knew she owned the second apartment as well, deliberately keeping it empty so she could have the entire floor to herself. She loathed the idea of a neighbour popping by to borrow a cup of sugar or gossip about the weather. This way she was able to maintain her privacy and retain some control over who visited.

After a short, smooth ride down to the lobby, Alice passed the reception desk and said hello to Kerry, the new Vanessa.

'Hi, Mrs Atkinson.'

Kerry was the same age as Vanessa, with short brown hair and freckles. Alice found her friendly enough but hadn't taken the time to get to know her.

'Settling in alright?'

'Oh yes, thanks. Greg and I are right at home.'

'Greg?'

Kerry picked up a small colourful figure from beneath her computer monitor. It was made of LEGO.

'Greg Gregorson from Gregville,' Kerry said with a bright smile. 'He goes everywhere with me.'

Alice frowned, then nodded politely and excused herself. It seemed age was the only thing Kerry had in common with Vanessa.

Alice stepped through the door marked Employees Only and proceeded down the hall to Tracey's office. She hesitated outside. It irked her to knock, especially because Tracey technically worked for her, but she understood it was the polite thing to do, so she gave the briefest of raps before pushing the door open.

Tracey was on the phone but gestured for Alice to take a seat.

'If you could look and let me know I'd appreciate it.'

Tracey hung up and smiled at Alice. It was the sort of smile that mingled friendliness with nervousness. 'Morning, Alice. How can I help you?'

'Tracey. Have you lost something?'

Tracey's eyes drifted to the phone on her desk and she sighed. 'I seem to have temporarily misplaced the master key-card. I know I had it this morning but now I can't find it. Not to worry,' she hurried on, 'I have staff looking for it. I'm sure it'll turn up.'

Alice's eyes narrowed as she considered telling Tracey that

FOUR

she thought she knew exactly where the key was. But she needed to be certain before making any accusations.

'Remind me, what does the master key-card open?'

Tracey fidgeted with a thin folder on her desk. 'It opens all the common areas, like the pool, the games room and gym, the dining room ... Don't worry, it doesn't provide access to residents' apartments.'

Alice adopted a satisfied look as if comforted by the manager's explanation. Inside she was doing a little dance for joy. She knew exactly what she'd seen.

'I'll let you get on with it then,' Alice said.

'Was there something you wanted, Alice?'

'Oh, not really. I was just wondering if you'd heard anything further from Rooproop Enterprises?'

Tracey shook her head. 'Not since you rejected their last offer a month ago.'

'Very good. Thanks.'

No longer interested in a walk, Alice considered this information on her way back to the lobby. Rooproop Enterprises had made several offers to buy Silvermoon, all of which Alice had rejected. As owner of the retirement village, she had fielded similar offers in the past, but this company was persistent. Despite several discrete enquiries, Alice hadn't managed to find out much about the company. If they came back again, she would be less discrete in asking around.

As she pressed the elevator button, she heard her name being called and turned to see Vanessa coming through the front door.

'That was quick,' Alice muttered.

'Doesn't take long if you know what you're doing,' Vanessa replied, 'and if the first person you run into has all the gossip.'

'Teresa,' Alice guessed. Teresa, a friend of Alice's, was a tremendous gossip.

Vanessa grinned. 'You got it. The new resident is arriving this afternoon. Her name is Sylvia Gregory, she's eighty-one and according to Teresa she must have good taste in furniture because she saw an antique side table being unloaded from the truck that was (and these are her words) "worth more than my ruby and diamond earrings".'

Vanessa broke off and looked at Alice expectantly.

'Five figures,' Alice informed her.

Vanessa whistled, which irritated Alice. She couldn't stand clichés.

The elevator doors slid open and they both stepped inside.

'What did you find out about the movers?'

'I had a chat to one of them. Said I was moving flats and was looking for a moving company. Harry said they were fully booked for the next six months.'

'Unlikely,' Alice said, 'but not impossible.'

Vanessa frowned. 'No, but there was something else. As I was leaving, I had a look at the logo on the side of the truck. It wasn't painted on. It was a sticker.'

'Unusual, but not impossible,' said Alice again. 'Perhaps a sticker was cheaper than painting?'

She unlocked the front door and sat in her armchair while Vanessa went into the kitchen. Alice hoped she wasn't going to brew more tea. She'd had more tea in the six years she'd been living here than the nine decades preceding it.

'Maybe,' Vanessa said. 'I would have thought it'd be cheaper and longer-lasting to have it painted on the side. Especially if they're so busy.'

She reached into the cabinet above the bench and pulled out

FOUR

a cereal box. She put her hand in and retrieved a small silver hip flask. She carried it over to Alice and flopped down on the couch.

'How did you know?' asked Alice.

'Was I wrong?'

Alice's response was to unscrew the flask and take a sip. The whisky inside had aged well.

'So what do we do now?'

Alice took another sip of whisky before replacing the lid on the flask. She told Vanessa about the missing key-card.

'Why didn't you tell Tracey what you saw?' Vanessa asked.

'I want to see what happens. How much was left in the truck for them to unload?'

Vanessa shrugged. 'A couple of big things and some boxes. They're probably done by now.'

'Good. Then we'll watch from here. If they stop to give the key-card back on their way out then we know one thing. If they don't, then we know something different.'

'Like what?'

Alice's eyes sparkled. 'Like…'

FIVE

Wellington, March 1994

'I didn't do it.'

Alice studied her granddaughter and nodded. 'As I said at school, I forgot to ask an important question. Was anything else taken from Helen Gregory's bag?'

'Why is that important?'

Alice tapped the driver on the shoulder and asked him to pull over. Amanda often asked why they didn't have their own car when they could afford it and she knew Alice could drive. Alice always replied that cars were a wasted investment. Amanda suspected there was more to it.

Alice paid the taxi driver and led Amanda to a bench overlooking the harbour. The day was overcast so there weren't many walkers or runners. A chilly wind swept off the water and Amanda pulled her jacket tighter.

'There is a famous saying that the only two things certain in life are taxes and death, or something like that. It's rubbish of course. There are many certainties in life. You will get hungry,

FIVE

tired, fall in love with the wrong person, and at some point during your life you will make an enemy. Do you understand?'

Amanda nodded.

'For most people, the word enemy is probably too strong. There will be someone who dislikes you, and whether you dislike them back or not is irrelevant. But there are occasions where it goes deeper than that. I asked if there was anything else missing from Helen Gregory's bag because if there was then there could be a third player in the game.'

'Game! I got called to the principal's office.'

'And nothing happened to you,' Alice said with a dismissive wave of her hand. 'It's possible someone took something from Helen's bag and to cover it up she planted several more items in your desk to divert suspicion. It's certainly not someone who likes you, so you can rule out your friends.'

'I don't have any friends,' Amanda said.

'Rubbish. What about that girl, what was her name, Mary? Genevieve?'

'Genevieve! We're not living in medieval times, Gran.'

'Don't call me that.'

'Her name is Marion.'

'Oh yes, not medieval at all.'

'And she's not talking to me because Helen told her to stay away.'

'She listened? What a weak-willed girl.'

A seagull drifted past on the wind, searching for dropped morsels of food.

'Yes, she listened. Helen is popular and I'm a weirdo.'

Alice's sigh was almost lost on the wind. 'Do you know who Gary Knightsbridge is?'

Amanda rolled her eyes and shook her head.

'Gary Knightsbridge was a singing sensation in the 1970s. He had six hit songs in a row.'

Amanda stared at her. 'You listened to music?'

'Very funny. Of course I did. Not that pop rubbish. Gary Knightsbridge sang ballads. When he toured the world, thousands of screaming girls greeted him in every city.'

'Were you one of them?'

'My dear, I was not then and never have been a screaming girl.'

'Did you have his poster on your wall? Have you got his albums at home? What—'

'Enough. My point is, Gary Knightsbridge was the most popular man on the planet. And then he wasn't. Last I heard, he was working in a fast-food shop in small town America.'

'So you're saying if I wait long enough Helen will start working at McDonalds?'

'Honestly, Amanda, have I taught you nothing?'

'Okay, sorry,' Amanda said with a grin. 'You're saying that popularity is fleeting so it shouldn't be important.'

'Precisely. This year Helen is a big fish at school, but next year when you go off to high school, she's going to be the tiniest fish around. If you let her affect you, you're wasting your time and energy. Understand?'

'I guess,' Amanda replied.

'Who else at school might have it in for you and/or Helen?'

Amanda scrunched up her face then shook her head. 'I can't think of anyone.'

Alice stood up and gestured for Amanda to follow. 'Tomorrow when you go back to school, you keep your mouth shut and your eyes open. Whoever it is will reveal themselves.'

'How can you be so sure?'

FIVE

'Because you're smart.'

'So is Helen.'

They walked back to the car and Alice paused with her hand on the door.

'Then let this be the lesson for the day. Always be the smartest person in the room, and if you can't, then be the most cunning. Do you understand?'

'Which one are you?' asked Amanda. 'The smartest or the most cunning?'

'Whichever is needed at the time.'

SIX

Wellington, August 2021

Alice and Vanessa stood at the window and watched one of the moving men emerge from the front door of the building and jump up into his truck.

'You don't know he was returning the key-card. He could have been telling Kerry they were leaving.'

'How much do you want to bet he was handing in the key-card that he found "lying on the ground"?'

Vanessa looked at her warily. 'I hate gambling with you. Anyway, there's an easy way to find out.'

She crossed to the landline on the kitchen bench and pressed the button that dialled the reception desk directly. She had a brief conversation and hung up. Her satisfied expression told Alice she'd been wrong.

'He was telling her they were done. Why were you so sure they'd taken the key-card?'

'A lifetime of assuming the worst of people.'

'That's kind of sad.'

SIX

Alice shrugged. 'It's pragmatic. I'm not saying I never trust anyone. You're here, aren't you?'

Vanessa strolled over to the patch of sun coming in through the window and stretched out on the floor.

'Have I got an assistant or a cat?' Alice grumbled.

'You've actually got both. What would those guys want with the key-card?'

'Apart from the obvious? I'm not convinced I am wrong. I suspect he's made a copy.'

'A copy? How? He's going to press the key-card into a bar of soap?'

'I doubt he'd use anything as rudimentary, but essentially yes.'

'What would you have used to copy a key?'

Alice mumbled a reply and when Vanessa asked again, she snapped, 'A bar of soap.'

When Vanessa started laughing, Alice reached down and picked up a padlock from under the couch. Vanessa's laugh turned to a groan as Alice handed it to her.

'You wouldn't need the bar of soap if you could pick a lock.'

'I've tried. This is an impossible lock. It simply can't be opened with anything but a key.'

Alice took the lock and reached for the lockpicks resting on the coffee table. Ten seconds later the lock clicked open. Without another word she relocked it and gave the lock and the picks to Vanessa.

'You're not normal,' Vanessa said.

'No, dear.'

'Anyway, a key-card is electronic. You couldn't copy it with a mould. You'd need specialist equipment.'

'Yes, I am aware of that. So let's leave that little mystery for the moment. While you open the padlock, I'm going to have a think.'

'Would it be wrong of me to hope there is something else going on?'

'Not at all,' replied Alice.

'Just no more murders. I'd be happy if I never saw another body again.'

A few hours later the padlock lay open on the coffee table and Vanessa had gone home for the day. The sun was lower and long shadows reached across the grass opposite the building. Someone was sitting in the rose garden. The angle meant Alice couldn't quite recognise who it was. She watched as a second woman emerged from the building and crossed to the bench. She had a brief conversation with the sitter and then they walked back into the foyer together.

Alice decided to take a gentle stroll around the gardens.

Stepping out into the warm evening, she was glad she'd brought a sweater. She had no doubt that Vanessa would be swanning around in a sleeveless blouse, but Alice had never had much "meat on her bones" (as her mother had liked to say) and with every passing year she found herself more sensitive to the cold.

To her left along the garden path was the indoor pool, gym and games room. There was an official name for the building but all the residents called it the Olympic complex. It was a somewhat ironic title considering the athleticism of most of the Silvermoon residents.

Alice peered through the front windows and saw an aqua jogging class in session. It was supposedly good exercise but Alice had never seen the point. If she was getting in the water,

SIX

it was with the objective of getting from one side to the other as quickly as possible. Aqua jogging seemed designed to do the opposite.

Beyond the Olympic complex was the small visitor carpark, and next to that was Charlie's Café where residents could get a caffeine fix without having to leave the grounds. Alice waved at Freda and Les who were sitting at one of the outside tables. They looked to be deep in conversation and didn't notice her. Alice smiled, wondering what hobby Les had decided to take up now. Since retiring, he'd embarked on a number of wildly different activities, all apparently with the point of proving he wasn't old. To date, his interests had included weight-lifting and choir-singing.

Alice headed towards the main residence for most Silvermooners, which was a large two-storey brick building at the rear of the retirement village. Like most buildings it had an official name, but residents just called it Stumpy. Longer and taller than the main building it had ten apartments on the ground floor. Her eyes went to the third door from the left. This had been the Iversons' apartment but there was no sign of the new occupant.

Alice had never been a 'welcome to the neighbourhood' sort of person, so knocking on the front door was out of the question. However, there were several bench seats next to the path and she made her way over to one of them and eased herself down. Her ankle was aching slightly but overall she was pleased with how well it had held up.

She'd waited long enough to feel she was wasting her time, and stood up to head home, when the front door of the apartment opened and two women stepped out. They spotted her instantly and the elder of the two gave a friendly wave.

Antiques and Assault

Alice took that as an invitation and made her way over to them.

'Welcome to Silvermoon,' Alice said.

'Thank you,' the older woman replied. 'I'm Sylvia and this is my granddaughter Helen.'

'I'm Alice. Nice to meet you.'

Helen frowned briefly when she heard the name. Alice saw the briefest moment of recognition cross her face before a smile masked any other emotion. Helen was in her late thirties or early forties, with dark shoulder length hair and too much make-up. She was dressed casually but immaculately and Alice wondered who she was trying to impress.

'Have we met before?' asked Helen.

'Oh dear, I'm not sure. Have we?' Alice replied. 'I'm sorry, I've met so many people in my life, I have trouble remembering these days.'

She watched Helen's shoulders relax and genuine warmth replace her fake smile. 'Perhaps not then. You just remind me of someone.'

'Forgive my granddaughter,' Sylvia said. 'She is very popular so assumes that she's met everyone and that they have met her.'

Helen shot her an irritated look which Sylvia met with a bemused one of her own. Sylvia's grey hair was neatly cut and she wore a crisply-pressed shirt and diamond earrings – it was a watered down version of Helen's smart casual look.

'My granddaughter is like that as well. Always thinking she's the smartest one in the room.'

'Does your granddaughter live here in town?' Helen asked.

'No, but she visits often.'

'That's good. So important to have family. When did you last see her?'

SIX

Alice pretended to think. 'Let me see now, what day is it today? I'm sure it wasn't that long ago.'

Helen abruptly turned to Sylvia. 'I'd better go. Come see me off Sylvia.'

It sounded more like an order than a request and Sylvia followed with an apologetic smile at Alice.

Alice followed them at a much slower pace. By the time she made it to reception, the two women were huddled beside a parked car on the driveway, deep in conversation.

She paused just inside the main doors, partially hidden by a concrete pillar. The conversation outside lasted a few more minutes, then Helen got into the car, slamming the door, and Sylvia strode back towards her apartment.

Alice thought there had been something peculiar about the interaction. But as she rode the elevator back to her floor, she began to wonder whether that was truly the case or if she had invented seeing the tension between them. Boredom could be hazardous.

There was nothing on television she wanted to watch. Amanda had signed her up for a range of new streaming thingies, but to Alice more choice made it harder to settle on something. She'd read every book on her shelves at least twice and had zero interest in learning to knit. What she needed was a good mystery to sink her teeth into.

She picked up her mobile phone and decided to call Amanda. Then she changed her mind and pulled up Vanessa's number, before changing her mind again and putting the phone back down. Alice never called just to chat. She had conversations, she gave instructions and sometimes orders, but she didn't chat. If she called them, Vanessa would overreact and Amanda would think Alice was losing the last of her marbles.

With a sigh, Alice closed her eyes and shuffled through her catalogue of memories. Helen had definitely recognised her, even though more than twenty five years had passed. If Alice had been working when they'd met, she might have felt annoyed by that. To be a good con artist one needed to be memorable when you wanted and utterly forgettable the rest of the time. However, Alice reasoned, she had been retired by the time she'd met Helen so ensuring her anonymity had no longer been a priority.

But that wasn't it. There was something else bothering her. The more she sought it out the more it eluded her, until she finally cornered the thought and dragged it into the light.

Helen had been relieved when Alice said she didn't recognise her. Was she relieved because of what had happened all those years ago, or because of something that was happening now? Alice cast her mind back. Perhaps it was all related to…

SEVEN

Wellington, March 1994

'...someone poisoned Mrs Kingston.'

Alice blinked. Of all the possible reasons Amanda could be sent home early from school, this hadn't made it onto her list.

'What do you mean poisoned?' Alice asked.

'What do you think I mean?' Amanda replied excitedly. She jiggled from one foot to the other like she was standing on hot coals. 'Miss Parker came in after lunch and said someone had poisoned Mrs Kingston – and she might die!'

Alice raised her eyebrows then grasped Amanda by the shoulder. All those short sharp movements were giving her a headache. 'Take a deep breath,' she said.

Amanda immediately complied.

'And another.'

By the time the second breath was exhaled, Amanda had stopped jiggling.

'Amanda, in any situation it is always the details that matter. There is a considerable difference between someone being

Antiques and Assault

accidentally poisoned by eating something bad and someone being deliberately poisoned with the intent of causing harm. Either way could be fatal and that is not a cause for celebration.'

Amanda's face fell. She slumped onto the beanbag next to the couch. 'It's not like I want her to die,' she muttered.

'What exactly did you hear?'

Amanda curled a strand of hair around her finger as she thought carefully.

'Miss Parker came in after lunch and said all afternoon classes had been suspended.' She paused for confirmation from Alice that she'd used the right word and continued after a small nod. 'She looked upset. She said that all our parents were being called and we had to wait for them in the front courtyard. Selwyn asked why we were getting the afternoon off – which I thought was stupid because you should never question getting an afternoon off school. Anyway, so Miss Parker said Mrs Kingston had been poisoned and that the police were coming.'

'Interesting. Are you sure that's exactly what she said?'

'Yes, why?'

'Because how would she know that Mrs Kingston had been poisoned and wasn't just sick?'

Amanda's eyes grew large. 'I don't know,' she admitted. 'But I don't think Miss Parker would say it if it wasn't true.'

'Sometimes adults are just like children, dear. They overreact, either out of excitement or a desire to be seen as important. Ask yourself which is more likely – that Mrs Kingston has food poisoning, or that someone tried to kill her?'

Amanda took some time to answer, then she sighed. 'The first one.'

Alice nodded. 'Right. Now, since you're not at school you

SEVEN

can do some more important homework. We're still working on locks so go get the box.'

Amanda protested all the way to the hallway cupboard where the box of locks was kept. She grumbled all the way back to the living room.

Half an hour later most of it was out of her system, when there was a knock at the door. Amanda raced out of the room before Alice could react.

Seconds later Amanda burst back into the room. 'The police are here.'

Alice's only reaction to this announcement was a raised eyebrow. Amanda found it both impressive and disappointing. It wasn't like the police visited every day.

At the front door two uniformed constables waited patiently.

'Alice Strong?' the younger of the two asked.

'Yes, officer. How can I help you?'

'We'd like to speak with you about your granddaughter Amanda and an incident which occurred at Roseneath Primary School today. May we come in?'

'Of course.'

She led them into the living room and waited until they were settled before offering them a drink, which they both declined. Amanda hovered next to Alice's chair.

'How can I help you?'

The older constable, a larger man with razor-short brown hair, pulled out a notepad.

Since they hadn't introduced themselves, Amanda automatically labelled the older one Big Copper and the younger Baby Copper.

'At approximately twelve o'clock today we were called to Roseneath Primary School to attend an incident. The principal,' Big Copper glanced down at the notepad, 'a Mrs Frances Kingston, had collapsed and was being treated by paramedics. They informed us that it appeared Mrs Kingston had been poisoned. We're currently having the contents of her coffee cup analysed.'

'That's terrible,' Alice commented.

'Yes,' he replied sternly. 'Attempted murder is terrible.'

'But I don't understand what this has to do with Amanda.'

'A witness saw your granddaughter leave the principal's office shortly before Mrs Kingston was discovered.'

'But that's not true! I didn't—'

Alice held up her hand and Amanda immediately stopped talking.

'Let me get this straight. You're accusing my granddaughter of … what? Trying to harm her school principal? Why?'

Both men shifted in their seats and exchanged a look. It seemed that their hopes of an easy conversation with a doddery old lady had been way off the mark.

'We understand Amanda was recently accused of stealing from another student's bag.'

'But I didn't do that.'

'You were questioned by Mrs Kingston yesterday?' said Baby Copper.

'Are you suggesting that in some form of retribution of being falsely accused of theft my twelve-year-old granddaughter concocted some plan to kill her principal?'

'That probably wasn't her intention,' replied Big Copper. 'She probably thought she'd just make her a little sick. Maybe teach her a lesson?'

'I didn't do anything!' Amanda yelled.

Alice turned her head and caught Amanda's eye. Amanda

SEVEN

took a deep breath, then another. Her face relaxed.

'Amanda, please leave the room.'

Amanda immediately stood and left the living room, closing the door behind her.

'We have more questions for her,' Big Copper protested.

Alice fixed him with an icy stare. 'Gentlemen, you have a job to do and my understanding is that your job is investigating, not fishing. If you have specific questions, then ask them. Otherwise you may go.'

Baby Copper looked like he was going to protest, but Big Copper put his hand on the other man's arm.

'We'll be back,' he said.

'You can see yourselves out.'

Alice waited until she heard the front door shut before saying, 'You can come out now.'

Amanda slunk in from the dining room. 'How did you know I was there?'

'Please.'

Amanda grinned, then looked worried. 'They don't seriously think I tried to kill Mrs Kingston.'

Alice drummed her fingers against the arm of her chair and examined her granddaughter thoughtfully. 'I don't believe they do. I suspect they think you were trying to make her sick and got carried away.'

'Gran!'

'Don't call me that,' Alice replied idly. 'I never said that's what I thought. But they can barely have had a chance to interview all the staff at school. Yet they came right here. Someone pointed them in your direction.'

'It's obvious,' Amanda said. 'Helen Gregory. She still thinks I nicked her stuff.'

'I wonder.'

'What are we going to do? Wait for them to come back and haul me off to jail?'

Alice blinked and shook her head slightly to bring her thoughts back into the room. 'Oh honestly. My dear, our family has never been to jail and we aren't going to start now, especially for something you didn't do. But sadly the police follow their guts more than their brains, so if we want this resolved, we'll have to do it ourselves.'

Amanda threw herself into Alice's arms. 'I love you,' she said.

Alice patted her on the shoulder and pretended to scowl.

'Yes dear, let's go.'

'Do you love me?'

'Do you feel loved?' Alice replied.

'Yes.'

'Then the words are irrelevant. Do you want to debate emotions or catch a poisoner?'

Amanda's face fixed with a determined look. 'Let's go,' she said. 'And if Helen Gregory set me up, she's going to be sorry.'

EIGHT

Wellington, August 2021

'How could you? She's beautiful.'

'What does beauty have to do with that?'

Alice pointed at the headless bird lying on the carpet. She'd grown accustomed to Maddy, the village cat, visiting her, although it had been a mystery for quite a while as to how the cat managed to navigate the elevator and the locked front door.

But this was taking her welcome too far.

'This is your fault,' Alice said.

'Mine or the cat?' Vanessa replied with a smile.

'Both! You're the one that sneakily lets her in here. Now she thinks she's welcome.'

'Relax, I'll clean it up. It's not like this is the first time she's brought you a present.'

'No but it'll be the last. She's banned from this apartment.'

Vanessa looked shocked. 'You can explain that to her while I get rid of the body.' Vanessa put the cat down on the coffee

Antiques and Assault

table then fetched a roll of paper towels from the kitchen with which to wrap the corpse. She scooped it up and carried it through the door to the downstairs dumpster in the parking lot.

Maddy looked at Alice and licked her lips.

Alice stared down at her, trying to get Maddy to look away first. When she eventually did it was in a casual way that implied she was bored, not cowed by Alice's scrutiny.

Vanessa took longer than expected to return from disposing of the bird. When she opened the front door, she found Maddy curled up on the couch next to Alice purring loudly.

'Not a word,' Alice warned her.

'Okay, first off, that's cute but you can't stop me thinking or saying it. And second, there's something going on outside.'

'I'm sure there are a lot of things going on outside. Be more specific.'

Vanessa crossed over to the window. 'There's an ambulance and a police car here at Silvermoon. Is that specific enough?'

Alice felt a shiver of concern as she joined Vanessa at the window. There were no emergency vehicles in sight.

'What are you talking about?'

'They're around the back, at the new lady's place.'

Alice sighed with relief. She hoped nothing serious had happened to Sylvia Gregory, but was relieved it wasn't any of her friends that the ambulance was here for.

'And ...?' Alice said.

'And ... I'm just going to see what I can find out. I thought you might like to come with me.'

Alice thought for a moment. 'No, you go and snoop. I might head to Charlie's for a tea and muffin.'

Vanessa gave her a shrewd look. 'Tea, a muffin and some

EIGHT

gossip.'

'Vanessa,' Alice said with a pained expression, 'I don't gossip. I gather intel.'

Charlie's was buzzing. All the outside tables were filled with people staring at the ambulance and police cars and trying not to be caught doing so.

Inside the café was just as busy. By the time Alice reached the counter and placed her order (a long black in a takeaway cup, a far weaker drink than the Turkish coffee she loved so many decades earlier, but about all her stomach could handle), she'd heard enough to realise the only topic being discussed was the arrival of the police and ambulance. She spotted Freda and Les in the front corner and carried her cup between the tables towards them.

'Hello, Alice,' Freda said. 'Join us please.'

'Any idea what's going on out there?' Les asked, pointing outside.

'I was just about to ask you the same question.'

Freda took a sip of her frothy cappuccino and dabbed chocolate from the corner of her mouth with a napkin. 'I heard from Teresa that Sylvia (I think that was her name, wasn't it Les?) I heard she was woken up in the middle of the night when an intruder viciously attacked her and left her lying in a pool of blood.'

'Who found her?'

Freda blinked. 'I don't know. But the ambulance showed up about twenty minutes ago.'

Alice looked out the window. A single constable stood at the entrance to the apartment. There was no sign of Vanessa.

'I'm starting to think Silvermoon isn't a safe place to live out

Antiques and Assault

my days after all,' Freda said.

'We're not moving,' replied Les firmly.

Alice didn't believe in coincidences. Someone being attacked the day after moving in almost definitely ruled them out as a random target. So, who was this Sylvia Gregory and why had someone come after her?

She spotted Vanessa walking towards the café, excused herself and met Vanessa outside. They headed to the nearest bench seat. From there they could still see the open front door of the apartment.

'Okay, so the story is that at seven this morning Gareth (he's one of the gardening crew) came in early to do some tidying up and noticed the front door of Sylvia's apartment was open. He knocked and looked inside and found Sylvia sitting in a chair, holding an ice pack to her head with her hand all bloody.'

'Not quite lying in a pool of blood then,' Alice said with a glance towards the café.

'What? Ew. No. Anyway, she told him someone had broken in and she'd managed to fight them off.'

'Impressive.'

'Gareth called the police and the ambulance and he stayed with her until they arrived.'

At that moment the door to the apartment opened and two paramedics came out carrying their bags. They were closely followed by two police officers and finally by Tracey.

'Quite a party,' Alice murmured.

Everyone got into their respective vehicles and drove slowly away down the driveway, while Tracey headed in the direction of her office on foot.

'I guess she wasn't hurt bad enough to warrant a visit to the hospital.'

EIGHT

Alice nodded.

'Should we go and talk to Sylvia?'

'Not yet. I want to check something first.'

They caught up to Tracey in the lobby where she'd stopped to talk to Kerry on reception.

'Ah, Alice. It's not a good time, I'm afraid. There's been an incident.'

'You can say assault. It won't offend my delicate nature,' Alice replied. 'Besides, that's precisely what I want to discuss. Shall we go to your office?'

She didn't wait for an answer, heading past the reception desk and down the hallway. Tracey caught up as Alice reached the office and Alice allowed Tracey to reclaim a resemblance of control by stepping aside and following her into her office.

Tracey sat down slowly behind her desk. 'What's this about?'

'The security cameras I had installed at the entrance. I assume you're getting the pictures for the police? I want to look at them first.'

Tracey hesitated.

Alice waved a hand impatiently. 'If I was nosier, I'd have kept the presence of the cameras to myself,' she said. 'I'm only interested in seeing the footage from last night.'

'Alice, despite what you may think, I don't dislike you. I'm not reluctant to show you out of obstinance or a sense of propriety or protecting the residents' privacy.'

'Why then?'

'I'm guessing you want to see it because you're planning on sticking your ... uh, you're planning to investigate the incident yourself. However, I'm aware that you've already put yourself at risk several times recently and frankly I'm concerned.'

Alice sat down in one of the visitor chairs and Vanessa took the other.

'For your job or my life?' Alice said. She quickly held up her hand. 'Don't answer that. It was rude. I apologise.'

Tracey looked astonished at the apology. By the similar expression on Vanessa's face it occurred to Alice that she'd perhaps not said sorry very much. It wasn't a habit she intended to cultivate.

'The camera footage?' Alice said.

Tracey tapped at her keyboard, then turned her computer screen around so they could see. The picture showed the front of the building they were sitting in. Alice knew the camera was located high on the wall, disguised as a light fitting. Its range covered the driveway, grass area and fence opposite the building, and the edge of the rose garden.

There was a date stamp at the bottom of the screen identifying that the footage was from 10.00pm the previous evening. The seconds slowly ticked over and the image didn't change.

'Any way to speed this up?' asked Alice.

'I can do it,' Vanessa jumped up and grabbed the mouse from under Tracey's hovering hand. She did something that Alice couldn't follow and suddenly the clock on the screen was going much faster. They zipped past midnight seeing nothing but the wind shaking the trees unnaturally fast. The rest of the night was similarly uneventful.

'Stop. Go back.' Something had caught her eye.

Vanessa paused the video and rewound a few minutes before playing it back at normal speed.

'There,' Alice pointed.

'It's a shadow,' Tracey said, squinting at the screen.

'A moving shadow,' Alice replied.

'I don't know, Alice. It could just be a branch in the wind.'

EIGHT

'Rewind it.'

They watched it once more. Alice wasn't sure what the others thought they were seeing, but to her there was clearly a shadow that started in the trees just inside the front gate and moved slowly along the edge of the building until it disappeared from sight.

'You think it's a person?' Vanessa asked dubiously.

'Look at the time stamp,' Alice answered. 'This mysterious shadow comes onto the property at five in the morning. Two hours later Sylvia is found by the gardener.'

'I should give this to the police,' Tracey said.

Alice nodded. 'Good idea. Although there isn't much on there to see. If they respond like you two did they're just as likely to dismiss it as nothing.'

'There's a detective coming shortly to talk to me. And I have to arrange for our nurse to visit with Sylvia, since she insists she doesn't need to go to the hospital.'

'How hurt is she?' asked Vanessa.

'More shaken up than injured, fortunately. She has a cut on her hand and a bruise on her face. Damn, that reminds me. I need to call her granddaughter.'

Alice signalled to Vanessa and they left Tracey dialling her phone.

'Why are you so sure it was a person on the video?' asked Vanessa as they crossed to the elevator.

'The movement was deliberate. I don't know if you've ever studied wind, but when it blows through things they don't move in a uniform way.'

'I've never thought about it. But it sounds like you have.'

'Dear, when you're trying to shoot a target from two hundred yards away it pays to know what the wind will do to your bullet.'

Vanessa stared at her in astonishment. 'Please tell me you were a hunter and not an assassin.'

They stepped out of the elevator and Alice unlocked her front door.

'Oh, I wasn't the one shooting. I was being shot at.'

Vanessa followed her inside and closed the door behind them. 'Okay, every time I think I've heard the most outrageous thing from you, you go and top it. Why was someone shooting at you?'

Alice walked to the window and peered down to the driveway. 'That's a story for another time. Right now we need to talk about Helen Gregory.'

NINE

Wellington, March 1994

'Helen Gregory?'

Amanda held her breath and hoped Miss Boland wouldn't ask why she wanted to know. Her feud with Helen was well known amongst the teaching staff. Although 'feud' was Alice's word. Amanda just found Helen an annoying pain in the butt.

'Her mother is keeping her out of school for a few days.'

Amanda glanced around the corridor. Students were on their way to their next class, and no one was paying her much attention.

'I hope she isn't sick like Mrs Kingston.' She was pleased with the slight quiver of fear she'd managed to get in her voice.

Miss Boland looked at her suspiciously. 'Shouldn't you be getting to class?'

'Yes, Miss Boland.'

Amanda trudged to her classroom and slumped down in her seat. She'd seen her grandmother manipulate conversations like that and come away with every piece of information she'd wanted with ease.

She struggled to pay attention to the lesson about symbiosis. Selwyn, quicker with volunteering than thinking, stuck up his hand with an answer that was quite clearly wrong. Amanda wanted to shout out the right one, but she bit her lip. Gran always said blending in was the greatest form of camouflage. If you're part of the pack no one pays attention to you and you can get away with just about anything.

Irritably she shoved a loose hair behind her ear and glanced at the empty desk where Helen Gregory was supposed to be sitting.

Her grandmother's voice popped into her head.

Take a breath.

Amanda instantly obeyed, taking in a deep breath and letting it out slowly.

And another one.

She did.

She felt her anger dissolve and her thoughts come into focus. She felt a smile twitch her lips. Even from another location, Alice was able to get into her head.

Okay, Amanda, work the problem. Helen is away from school. Why? Option one, she's guilty. Option two, she's sick as well. Option three, she's a lazy little sod and has conned her mother into thinking she was upset by what happened at school.

Amanda's eyes slid around the classroom and came to rest on the one person who might have some answers – Helen's best friend in the whole world, Jenny Bailey.

Because she was Helen's friend, Jenny didn't like Amanda. In fact, she'd only said about eleven words to her since Amanda had started the previous term. Amanda understood dislike by

NINE

association. Alice didn't like spinach, so Amanda didn't like it either.

She found Jenny in the playground at lunchtime. The girl was sitting under a tree, eating by herself, when Amanda wandered up to her

'Hey, Jenny,' she said, as if surprised to see her there.

Jenny nodded and mumbled a response through a mouthful of sandwich. Amanda plonked down on the bench next to her and pulled out her own lunch. She frowned at her chocolate muffin and strawberry jam sandwich and silently wished Alice put as much effort into food as she did into preparing for a job.

She took a tiny bite of the sandwich, then offered the muffin to Jenny.

'Want to split this?'

Jenny's eyes widened and she started to reach out a hand, then stopped herself.

'It's okay, I don't feel like the whole thing.'

Amanda tore the muffin in half and offered some to Jenny. She hesitantly took it, staring at the muffin like it was made of poison. Amanda took a big bite and grinned a chocolatey grin. Reassured, Jenny took a bite of her piece and they ate in silence for a while.

'It's weird what happened to Mrs Kingston, eh?' Amanda said.

'Yeah. I heard it was a ham sandwich that she'd had in her desk drawer for a week.'

Amanda blinked. She hadn't heard that one, although there were some wild rumours flying around. Some might be close to the truth, while others (like the one started by Selwyn that Mrs Kingston had been poisoned by a ninja on the orders of a secret underworld boss determined to destroy the school) seemed less likely.

'You don't think the same thing that happened to Mrs Kingston has happened to Helen, do you?' she asked.

Jenny looked horrified and Amanda shrugged.

'I just mean it's weird that she's away today. I hope she's okay.'

'But you two hate each other.'

'Yes I don't like her,' Amanda admitted. 'But that doesn't mean I want her to die.'

'I literally heard you say I hope you die to her last week.'

'Well sure, but it's not like I meant it. That's just something you say.'

Jenny shook her head. 'Not me.'

Aren't you a saint.

'No, I guess not,' Amanda said softly. She wanted to say something else. To make some comment about how she and Helen had buried the hatchet, but again Alice's lessons came to mind. Sometimes silence will get you more information than words.

Amanda finished her half of the muffin and had just decided that Alice didn't know what she was talking about, when Jenny spoke.

'Helen gets migraines. That's probably what's happened today. She'll be back in a couple of days.' Jenny stood up, brushed crumbs off her skirt, and walked away without another word.

'Charming,' Amanda muttered.

Maybe Helen did have a migraine. But then why did Miss Boland say her mother was keeping her out of school? She didn't say she was sick. She'd said Helen's mother was keeping

NINE

her home. So maybe it wasn't a migraine at all. Maybe there was another reason. Like guilt.

So how could she prove it? Amanda abruptly stood up and marched across the playground.

The school office was down one end of the main building. It was comprised of a front desk, a photocopier, a tiny sick bay off to one side, and the principal's office down a short corridor. Amanda was surprised to see there wasn't a police officer standing outside Mrs Kingston's office door. She'd assumed it would be a crime scene.

'What can I do for you, Amanda?' asked Mrs Ferris. A large lady in her mid-fifties, with wavy brown hair and glasses, Mrs Ferris ruled the school office with a friendly smile and an iron hand. Nothing happened in the school without her knowledge. She was a perfect source of information. Unfortunately, she'd worked at the school for twenty years and had a heightened sense of intuition concerning student behaviour. Amanda hadn't had much to do with her before, but everyone in the school knew you never tried to put one over Mrs Ferris. Want to pretend you're hurt or sick? She'd seen it all before and had (what Alice called) enough sympathy not to be a female dog but not so much that she was taken in by every sob story that passed her desk. Amanda had had to think about the first part of that before she'd understood.

'I—'

The desk phone rang and Mrs Ferris held up a finger to indicate Amanda should wait while she answered it.

'What do you mean you're here now? Delivery wasn't due until 2pm. Fine, I'll be right there.' She slammed the phone down and stood up with a scowl. 'Wait here a moment, Amanda. This won't take long.'

Once she was gone, it took Amanda several moments to realise this was her chance. Glancing around to make sure she was alone, she quickly walked to Mrs Kingston's office and slipped through the door. It looked identical to the last time she'd been there. She crossed to the desk, not sure what she was looking for. The computer screen was blank and the desktop was a mess of papers. She sat in the chair and thought, all the time watching the door. She expected it to burst open at any moment and the police to drag her away to jail.

She took a deep breath, then another, and finally one more. Her thoughts came into focus. The last time she'd been in here, she'd seen Mrs Kingston check something in her desk calendar.

Quickly she searched through the papers, finally finding the calendar on the corner of the desk. The day before Mrs Kingston had had appointments all morning and all afternoon, except for the hour just before lunch. There had been an appointment filled in for that time but it had been crossed out. She couldn't make out who it had been with.

'Think, Amanda,' she muttered. 'What would Alice do?'

She held the page up and could faintly make out something beneath the scribble, but it was too faint. She switched on the desk lamp and held up the paper in front of it. Whoever had crossed the name out had done a good job. All she could make out was an A and a T.

She put the diary back where she'd found it and stood up. She was halfway to the door when it opened.

'What are you doing!'

TEN

Wellington, August 2021

'We were terribly upset to hear about your intruder and wanted to make sure you were alright,' Alice replied.

Sylvia Gregory looked surprised, then stepped back to let Alice and Vanessa inside. 'Thank you. It's been a terrible shock.'

Alice had expected to find a mess of half-unpacked boxes, but the place was spotless, as if Sylvia had lived there for years. The furniture all looked new, with the exception of a wooden side table and a wooden chair in the corner of the living room. In contrast all the small items on the table and bookshelves looked old. Before Alice could study them more closely, they were offered tea.

'No, thank you Sylvia, but we brought you a muffin from Charlie's,' Alice replied. 'That's the café just across the way. We thought you might have been too busy unpacking to think about food. But I can see we were wrong.'

Sylvia looked around with a hint of pride on her face. 'Oh, I don't like the clutter of boxes. I make sure to unpack as soon as I move into a new place. You get it down to an art form when you've moved as many times as I have. Sorry, I didn't catch your names.'

'Silly me,' Alice replied with a smile. 'My name is Alice. We met yesterday. And this is Vanessa.'

'Your granddaughter?'

'No, my assistant.'

'Oh, I see.'

Sylvia motioned for them to sit on the couch while she perched on the edge of a single seater facing the window. She had a dark bruise on her cheek and a bandage around her left arm.

'We just wanted to reassure you that Silvermoon is a safe place. I feel terrible that something like this could happen here,' Alice said. 'And so soon after you moved in.' She shook her head in disbelief.

'Well, thank you for saying that. I must admit that I've been wondering if I wouldn't be safer moving straight out again.'

'I hope you don't think it was someone at Silvermoon who attacked you.'

Sylvia's eyes widened and her hand flew to her mouth. 'I hadn't even … do you think it was?'

'Absolutely not,' replied Vanessa.

'Is your granddaughter going to come back and see you today? It's so important to have loved ones close after something upsetting.'

Alice caught the amused look that crossed Vanessa's face. No doubt she was thinking that when Alice had experienced worse scenarios the last thing she'd wanted was people around her. She preferred one of the hip flasks hidden around her apartment and her own company.

TEN

'Yes, my Helen will be here this afternoon. She went out of town on business yesterday and is flying straight back.'

'What does she do for a job?' asked Vanessa.

'Oh dear, I'm not entirely sure,' Sylvia replied with a tiny laugh. 'She has explained it to me but it's so complicated. Something to do with money.'

Alice stifled her irritation. Few things annoyed her more than the clueless old lady thing. She forced a smile. 'I know what you mean. I never know what my granddaughter is doing from one day to the next. So you've moved a few times?'

Sylvia nodded. 'This is the last time, god willing. I'm too old and too tired to keep this up.' Sylvia sank back into her chair, looking tired. 'I do hope they catch the man, but I didn't even get a good look him. He had this mask thing over his face. And he wore gloves and a jacket.'

Alice felt a twinge of sympathy.

'What did he want?'

Sylvia looked at Vanessa in amazement. 'My jewellery, of course.'

Out of habit, Alice had scanned Sylvia and her home for anything of value on her way in. Sylvia's earrings were small diamonds and the stones in her two rings were so small they were hardly worth stealing.

'Can you tell the police what he sounded like?' Alice said. 'That might help.'

'I don't know. All he said was "Where is it?". It was so sudden it was hard to focus on his voice.'

'You poor thing. How scary,' Vanessa said. 'Is that all he said? I wonder what *it* was?'

'I honestly don't know. I tried to ask, but I was too frightened to speak.' Sylvia looked like she was about to burst into tears.

Antiques and Assault

'You were so brave to fight him off,' Alice said quickly.

Sylvia gave a deep breath and a wan smile. 'I managed to pick up a vase and hit him over the head with it. Such a shame. It was old and I think Helen will be upset it's broken. But he let go and ran away out the door.'

Alice nodded. She was all for affirmative action against people trying to hurt her.

'So he didn't take anything?' asked Vanessa.

Sylvia shook her head.

'Well, we should let you rest. If you need anything, please let me know. Ask at reception and they'll direct you to my apartment.'

'Thank you.'

They didn't speak until they were halfway back to Alice's place.

'Well, what do you think?'

'What do you think?' Alice repeated back to her.

Vanessa thought for a moment. 'She seemed to be in shock. It sounded like a horrible experience.'

'But?'

'But something didn't sit right with me.'

'Such as?'

'I can't put my finger on it. So how about you tell me what I missed?'

Alice patted her arm. 'You picked up that something wasn't right, so that's a good start. As for the rest, there was nothing specific, just little things that didn't add up. In my line of work, it's important to calculate the odds; what is the likeliness of the story being true? That assessment often means the difference between success and failure.'

'Okay, I get that, but how does that relate to this?'

TEN

They waved to Teresa who was going into the Olympic complex carrying a bag. Alice knew her friend swam several times a week.

'The obvious question is what are the odds that someone would be attacked on their first night in a new residence? And then what are the odds that Sylvia would be randomly selected as a target?'

'I guess the answer to both of those is pretty slim.'

'Don't guess, dear. It makes you sound uncertain.'

'I am uncertain.'

'But it never pays to let people know that.'

Vanessa sighed. 'Fine. The answer to both is they're unlikely.'

'Highly unlikely. Then, add in that the intruder was after something specific – he kept asking her where it was.'

They climbed the steps and went into the foyer.

'That could have just been a ploy. Keep asking for something vague and eventually they'll tell you where something valuable is.'

'Indeed, and a most inept way of doing things. Imagine not going into a place with a firm item in mind.'

'Your problem is that you think everyone is as skilled as you were. Uh, are.'

'No, my problem is assuming no one is as skilled as me. Remember – be the smartest in the room, and if you can't then …'

'… be the most cunning. But I'm not very cunning.'

'Of course you are. You're a woman. We're born with a natural amount of cunning. It's like any other skill – you're not going to get better unless you train. I remember a particularly painful lesson with Amanda when she was …'

Alice trailed off as she opened the front door of her apartment and they walked inside.

'I'm going to need you to finish that sentence,' Vanessa said.

'Oh sorry. When she was twelve. The last time we had Helen Gregory in our lives – before now that is.'

'But she's not really in your life now. Tea?'

Alice sighed and settled herself onto the couch. 'Fine.'

'It's her grandmother who's living here.'

'So let's focus on her. See what you can find out about Sylvia Gregory.'

'Got it. What are you going to do?'

'I need to talk to Amanda. I don't recall meeting Sylvia before at all, but Amanda might have some memory of her.'

Vanessa finished making the tea, then headed downstairs to see what she could find out about Silvermoon's newest resident.

Meanwhile Alice tried to reach Amanda. She got her answerphone and left a message. 'Call me,' she ordered.

She drank her tea by the window. As her joints began to tell her she'd spent too long standing in one spot, she recognised the car from yesterday slowly cruising up the driveway. It pulled into the visitor carpark next to the Olympic complex and a woman got out. Was it Helen Gregory? Alice's eyesight was better than most of her friends and, if she believed her doctor, was better than it should have been at 98. Even so, she wasn't sure at this distance. She squinted. The woman was holding something. It could have been a handbag, or it could have been a birthday cake with sparklers for all Alice could see.

As she watched, a sudden thought came to her. She made her way into the hallway, down the elevator and out of the building where, instead of turning right into the Silvermoon

TEN

grounds, she turned left towards the driveway and front gate.

The driveway was paved, with grass on either side. There was no reason for anyone to walk there unless they were a gardener or someone wanting to be sneaky. There was no evidence of the early morning visitor.

Alice closed her eyes and replayed the surveillance footage in her mind. The figure had been creeping along the trees on the right-hand side of the driveway. She peered down at the grass. Like everywhere else, it was kept well-trimmed. Alice had never paid much attention to it before, but it looked almost like someone had gotten down on hands and knees and snipped every blade with a pair of scissors and a ruler. That meant there were no footprint impressions.

She walked from the gate to the trees and couldn't see anything that might be useful. Not discouraged, Alice went back to the gate and stepped onto the grass again, this time searching around the trees themselves, looking for any other sign of the early morning intruder.

Four steps from the gate she noticed something caught on a low tree branch. Carefully she pulled free a scrap of material. Alice was a tad shorter than most people and it was caught slightly above the level of her pants pocket.

The ragged piece of grey material meant nothing to Alice. She didn't remember seeing a torn pocket, and any thief worth their salt would have ditched the clothes they were wearing.

The colour of the fabric didn't match the garden crew at Silvermoon anyway, they wore a dark green uniform.

She brought the fabric to her nose and sniffed. She caught a familiar smell of tobacco. Alice had tried smoking during the sixties. Everyone was doing it and for a while you were considered a social pariah if you didn't have a cigarette between your fingers. But she'd never felt comfortable with it. Now whenever doctors ask if she smoked, she smugly replied 'not since 1968', knowing that she'd smoked her last cigarette before most of them had even been born.

Knowing the intruder was a smoker wasn't much help but it was one more thing she didn't know before.

Alice smiled as she walked back to her apartment. There was nothing like a puzzle to solve to keep her brain running on all cylinders, and she was collecting information so quickly she was confident she'd have this whole situation wrapped up in no time.

ELEVEN

Wellington, March 1994

'Your granddaughter was caught in a restricted area.'

'A restricted area?' Alice repeated. 'That sounds official. Wasn't she found in Mrs Kingston's office?'

Mrs Ferris frowned. She wasn't used to being questioned. 'Exactly, and she had no right being there.'

'I'm sure she has a perfectly sensible explanation.'

'It doesn't matter what explanation she has.'

'Oh, so you haven't asked her?' Alice replied.

Mrs Ferris' frown deepened. 'No, I haven't,' she admitted.

The two adults turned to look at Amanda who'd been sitting quietly ever since she'd been caught.

'I was waiting out here for you, Mrs Ferris, like you said I should. But I wasn't sure how long you were going to be and we had a math quiz after lunch which I wanted to study for because math isn't my best subject …'

Alice gave the tiniest shake of her head and Amanda took a deep breath and smiled brightly.

'Anyway, when I was in Mrs Kingston's office with my grandmother I accidentally left my math book in there. Well, I thought I must have because it wasn't in my bag, so I thought I'd just take a look. I didn't want to waste your time.' She clamped her mouth shut and kept her eyes on Mrs Ferris.

'There, like I said, a perfectly sensible explanation.'

'She still shouldn't have been in there,' Mrs Ferris replied.

'I agree, and I'll have a word with her about going where she's not supposed to. But it's not like the office is a crime scene?'

She phrased it as a question and Mrs Ferris reluctantly nodded.

'That's true enough. Although it should be. Someone meant to do her harm that's for sure.'

'Amanda, why don't you go back to class,' Alice said.

Amanda looked like she was going to argue. Instead she mumbled something under her breath and stomped out of the office. She stopped just outside the slightly ajar door and listened carefully.

'I do apologise for her.'

'That's perfectly alright. Raising her alone must be difficult.'

Amanda gritted her teeth.

'We manage. I do hope that Amanda hasn't added to any stress you must be feeling. Such a horrible accident to happen to Mrs Kingston.'

'Accident! Not likely. That was deliberate.'

'Surely not,' Alice replied in shock. 'I thought she was quite well-liked. Why would someone want to hurt her?'

'Well, there's the trouble with your granddaughter for a start. I told the police.'

Amanda decided it was time to talk to Alice again about

ELEVEN

moving schools. It was either that or she was going to have to do something about Mrs Ferris.

'Yes, it was quite right for you to do that.'

'I'm glad you think so. I feared you might be upset.'

'Why would I be upset? I'd rather the police rule out Amanda as a person of interest at the beginning. Very sensible if you ask me. But I do have to ask,' Alice continued, 'why are you so sure it wasn't an accident? Mrs Kingston is a primary school principal. I cannot believe she has an enemy who would want to do her such serious harm.'

'You'd be surprised, Mrs Strong. Some of the things I've seen in this office. Some parents can't face the fact that their little Selwyn isn't a genius. We get all sorts and some of them have nasty tempers.'

'I'm impressed that you're able to remain so calm. I don't think I would like being yelled at.'

'Oh it's not all that often really,' Mrs Ferris smiled. 'Most people we get through here are as pleasant as can be.'

'Well, I must dash, I'm getting my hair done in the city,' Alice said. 'And don't you worry, I'll have a strong word to Amanda about going places she's not supposed to.'

And getting caught!

Amanda hurried out of sight before Alice could exit the office. She needed to work out what was going on. She knew that the last thing Alice would want was the police sniffing around her life in general and home in particular. Alice always said that she wasn't a thief, she just persuaded people that she should own things that belong to them, mostly without paying for them. There were a few items around the house that a well-informed police officer might find interesting.

Antiques and Assault

Alice was waiting for her at the gate when school finished. 'What did you learn today?'

'We really did have a math test.'

'I mean real things, important things. What did you learn?' Alice repeated.

Amanda thought about this as they started towards the car. Finally she said, 'Mrs Ferris likes being in charge. She wants to know everything that's going on.'

'Why?'

'Because,' Amanda replied slowly, 'she wants to be important?'

Alice started to shake her head, then changed it to a nod. 'There are two reasons someone wants to be important. What might they be?'

'I don't know.'

'I don't expect you to *know*. But I expect you to form an opinion. Remember, the answer is the same whether someone is fifty or twelve.'

The driver was waiting for them at the curb. He was the same driver as the day before, but the car was different.

'So Helen Gregory could be the same as Mrs Ferris?'

'That depends on your answer to my question.'

Amanda pondered this all the way home. The car dropped them at the bottom of the hill where they boarded the small open-aired cable car that slowly carried them up to their house.

This was her favourite of all the houses they'd lived in. She liked to sit in the front room and stare down at the harbour. It was especially exciting when there were sail boats on it. Alice liked the house because it was hard for someone to sneak up on them. Depending on where you were in the house you could usually hear the cable car motor announcing guests.

ELEVEN

At the front door, Amanda split off to her bedroom, returning a few minutes later having replaced the school uniform with something more her style.

'People want to be important because inside they don't feel like they are.'

Alice paused with the freezer door open. She held up a chicken frozen meal in one hand and a pasta meal in the other.

Amanda pointed to the pasta one and Alice put the other back inside and closed the door.

'So why would people who don't feel important go to so much effort?' asked Alice.

'Because ... because they think it will give them something. Something that's missing in their life.'

Alice beamed at her granddaughter.

'Helen doesn't like me. She tries to make herself seem important by making me feel unimportant, because ... she's missing something?'

'Exactly. Why is it important for you to know that?'

'Because I can use that against her.'

Alice winced at hearing one of her lessons parroted back to her.

'Yes, that's true, but more than that. If you know it's about her and problems in her life, then she can't hurt you here.' She touched Amanda's forehead with her finger. 'Or here.' She touched her heart. 'That gives you a lot of power.'

Amanda took a bite of an apple and traced some letters on the counter top with her finger.

'What are you doing?'

She told Alice about the crossed out appointment and the two letters she was able to make out.

'A and T. Could be anything, but it's important, don't you

think?'
'I think we need to find out a bit more.'

TWELVE

Wellington, August 2021

'You're young. You've got plenty of time to move around,' Alice replied.

Vanessa looked at the small piece of paper on her hand and shook her head. 'Maybe. But I've lived in two places my whole life and she's lived in six different retirement homes in the last two years. Why would anyone move around that much?'

'Perhaps she hasn't found the right place yet,' suggested Alice. The years she'd been at Silvermoon were the most she'd spent in one place her entire life. 'It's not always easy to find the spot where you're going to be comfortable living for the rest of your life.'

'I guess not everyone can buy a retirement village,' Vanessa said with a grin.

Alice shrugged.

'But look at this, Auckland, Christchurch, Rotorua, Hamilton, and two different places in Wellington. She can't even settle on a city let alone a place to live.'

'That does seem unusual.'

Alice tried to recall whether any of her friends had talked about where they lived before moving to Silvermoon. They probably had. She had a vague memory of Freda saying that she and Les had lived in the same house … somewhere … for sixty years.

'But it doesn't necessarily mean anything. Maybe she's fussy. That doesn't tell us why she was targeted.'

'No,' Vanessa admitted. 'But like you always say, it's about knowing more than you did before.'

Alice laughed. 'Nice to know you're paying attention. And you're right, even though it's unlikely to be related it does tell us something about her character.'

'Right. The only other thing I could find out was that her granddaughter Helen is her emergency contact. I mean we could probably have guessed there was no husband because he's not here, but Sylvia's kids must be gone as well.'

'Not necessarily. Perhaps her children have their own health issues, or live in another part of the world, or don't get on with their mother. Just because they're not on some form doesn't mean they're dead.'

Vanessa looked down at piece of paper again, then shoved it in her pocket.

'I never asked about … Is … I mean … You never …'

'Is my daughter dead? Yes. Amanda's mother was killed in a car accident when Amanda was two years old.'

Vanessa shifted in her chair and awkwardly picked at a frayed patch on the knee of her jeans.

'It's alright, dear, it was a long time ago. And I've got Amanda.'

'It's just, you never talk about her. What was her name?'

TWELVE

Alice closed her eyes and took a deep breath. The pain of a memory from almost four decades ago came flooding back. She took another breath and felt it slide away just as quickly. A third breath banished it back into the vault. When she opened her eyes again Vanessa was watching her closely.

Alice smiled and said, 'Somethings are off limits.'

'I'm so sorry Alice, I didn't—'

'No, you didn't. Now, I have one more piece of information to share with you.' She told Vanessa about the clue she'd found in the trees.

'Shame we can't get it analysed,' said Vanessa.

'We're not trying to prove anything in court,' Alice reminded her. 'All that "this fibre came from the pocket of a six-foot left-handed man with a limp, who smokes a certain type of cigarette that is only sold in one shop in the whole of Wellington" is absolutely rubbish.'

'So you're saying we shouldn't rely on DNA or fingerprints to lead us to the culprit.'

'I'm saying don't use the word culprit. We're not talking about a cat that ate a bird,' Alice glared at the spot on the carpet where Maddy had left the bird corpse.

'The only way to solve a puzzle is by using your brain. You don't need a laboratory for that.'

'Then I guess we're lucky we have your brain on our side.'

'And yours,' Alice replied sharply. 'You don't do yourself any good downplaying your intelligence.'

'I wasn't. I'm smart. But you're smarter.'

'Not at your age I wasn't. I was definitely more cunning, but I was living through a world war. If I wanted to get anywhere as a woman, I needed cunning. But I didn't have the book smarts.'

'I didn't go to university either,' Vanessa replied.

'No and I never asked you why not. You could have done anything you wanted. Why were you working on reception at a retirement village?'

Vanessa shrugged. 'I didn't know what I wanted to do and didn't want to go to university for the sake of it. Most of my friends who graduated are in jobs that have nothing to do with their degree. It seemed like a waste.'

'Hmph. The only waste is not using the intelligence you've been given.'

'I'm here aren't I?'

Alice held her gaze and was pleased when Vanessa didn't look away. That was one of the reasons she'd persuaded the young woman to come and work for her. She was wasting her smarts at reception and there was a risk that Vanessa would amble through her life without achieving anything.

'Enough sentimentality—'

'That's sentimentality?'

Alice continued, pretending she hadn't been interrupted. 'Let's work on the basis that Sylvia Gregory was targeted specifically. Who knew she had moved here?'

Vanessa shrugged again. 'How are we supposed to know that? The list could be huge. Friends, family, her bank, NZ Post, Inland Revenue, old neighbours. Take your pick.'

Alice waved her hand impatiently. 'I'm starting to rethink calling you intelligent. Think about that list and tell me why none of them should be on it.'

Vanessa took a few moments then her eyes widened. 'Alright, so assuming government departments and banking corporations haven't taken to breaking into people's homes and attacking them, that wipes them off. Friends and family would

TWELVE

have known where she lived before so it would be weird for them to suddenly launch an attack. That leaves her old neighbours. Maybe Sylvia saw something or stole something from one of them.'

'Plausible. But there's a group of people you're missing.'

'Who?'

'Think, Vanessa. Who knew for sure that Sylvia was now living at Silvermoon, and which apartment she was in?'

'The movers,' Vanessa blurted out. 'I can't believe how dense I am. They shifted her stuff in so they knew where she lived and what sort of stuff she had. But wait …'

'Go on.'

'Sylvia said her attacker kept asking where *it* was. If they'd moved her belongings in then they'd know the location of whatever they were looking for.'

'Agreed,' Alice replied. 'So that leaves us with two possibilities. One, that it was one of the movers but they didn't know where she'd put the item. Or two, it wasn't them.'

'I'm sure the movers would be first on the police's list of suspects.'

'Undoubtedly. Should we just sit back and let the police handle it?'

'We should,' Vanessa agreed. 'But we're not going to, are we?'

'It's a matter of perception and a little pride. Freda told me today that she was wondering if Silvermoon was a safe place to live out her days. I can't have people thinking I'm letting them live in danger.'

'But no one knows you own the village.'

'I know. But I've never relied on the police for anything and I'm not about to break a habit of a lifetime now. If you want something done right …'

'Do it yourself?' Vanessa finished.

Alice snorted. 'No. Get me to do it.'

Vanessa bit her lip. 'What's our first move then, boss?'

'You practice,' Alice pointed to the box in the corner of the room, 'while I think.'

Vanessa retrieved the box and pulled out a padlock. 'You know, I don't think I've ever seen you open any of these. Maybe you need practice as well.'

Vanessa held the lock out as a challenge.

It wouldn't hurt to remind the girl why Alice was the teacher. She took the lock offered and waited for Vanessa to select another one. The two women stared at each other. Then Vanessa snatched a lockpick off the table.

'I'm going to beat you this—'

'Done,' Alice said.

Vanessa's head snapped up and she stared in disbelief at the open lock sitting on Alice's lap.

'How did you…'

Alice gestured to the closed lock in Vanessa's hand. Vanessa went back to working on it and twenty seconds later it clicked open.

'Very good, dear. A new record.'

Vanessa grinned. 'Thanks.'

'But remember most locks are on the outside of things, in the open, exposed. The longer you take to pick it the greater the chance you'll be discovered.'

'You couldn't have just left it at good job?' she muttered.

'Do you want a gold star? Maybe a pat on the back and an *atta girl*?'

'*Atta girl*?'

Alice's face split into a wide smile. 'The day you get an *atta*

TWELVE

girl out of me is the day they carry me out of here in a box. It's obvious I'm not going to get any thinking done with you here, so why don't you go elsewhere and do some research.'

'On what?'

'On the moving company.'

THIRTEEN

Wellington, March 1994

'Who brings a dog to a home for cats?' Amanda blinked and cocked her head to the side, unaware that she was imitating one of the animals.

'Don't do that, dear. I'll admit it's not a well-known saying, but it used to be.'

'Who's the sort of person who brings a dog to a home for cats?' Amanda repeated. 'What does that mean?'

'What do you think it might mean?' asked Alice.

Amanda straightened her head and chewed on the end of her hair.

'Don't do that, dear,' Alice said again. 'It's a tell, and whether you're playing poker or persuading a man that his diamond ring would look better on your finger, tells lead to failure.'

Amanda dropped the strand of hair and sucked on her lip instead.

'Then how am I supposed to think?' she complained when Alice pointed to her mouth.

THIRTEEN

'With your brain not your body.'

'Fine. You're talking about someone who doesn't care what everybody else thinks.'

Alice nodded. 'Almost, but more than that. It refers to someone who is malicious. Do you know what that means?'

'*Malicious*. Evil or spiteful.'

'Excellent. So someone who brings a dog to a home for cats knows that their actions will cause chaos but they do it anyway. We need to establish whether the person who poisoned your principal did it to kill her or cause chaos.'

'What difference does it make? She was still poisoned,' Amanda replied.

'It makes quite a bit of difference. The first intention would mean Mrs Kingston is wanted dead, the second would mean they simply wanted her out of the way.'

'She's out of the way if she's dead too.'

'That's correct, but one's more permanent than the other. Besides it's no small thing to kill a person.'

Amanda frowned. 'Okay, let's say someone wanted her out of the way. Why?'

'I think we can safely assume that it's related to school in some way rather than her personal life,' replied Alice. 'So why would someone want the principal away from school?'

'I don't know. I'd get it if it was a teacher, like we've got this science test coming up and if our teacher wasn't there then we wouldn't have to have it. But principals don't … I don't really know what they do. Mrs Kingston comes to assembly and tells us stuff, and you have to go to her office if you get in trouble.' Amanda shot Alice a wry smile. 'Or if someone tries to get you in trouble. But I don't know what they do all day.'

'In my day the role of a principal involved a strap or cane, but I'm pretty sure they aren't allowed to do that anymore. If they're anything like the head of a company then their job is to make decisions regarding how things run.'

'Cool.'

'Don't say cool.'

'Everybody says it.'

'You are not everybody, you are my granddaughter.'

'Gran—'

'And definitely don't say that.'

'You're so weird.'

'Thank you, dear.'

'That's not a ... argh! Talking to you is so frustrating.' Amanda stormed out of the room, slamming the door after her.

She went into her bedroom and slammed that door as well. Sometimes she wished she could go to boarding school and have a normal upbringing. She was pretty sure none of the other kids from school were taught to assess the value of things in a room when they walk in.

When she calmed down, she decided that weird though it was, she actually liked her life. She was holding onto that thought when the front doorbell rang. Alice and Amanda reached the front door at the same time.

On the doorstep stood two police officers, different from yesterday. A gray-haired man in a suit and a young fresh-faced constable.

'Mrs Strong? I am Detective Graves of Wellington CIB and this is Constable Wilson. May we have a word?' He said it with the practiced ease of an experienced police officer, mostly a request with a hint of insistence.

'Of course, Detective,' Alice replied with an open smile.

THIRTEEN

She led them through to the living area and then because she remembered that's what grandmothers were supposed to do, she offered them tea and biscuits.

'No, thank you,' Detective Graves replied. 'We're here to talk to you about your granddaughter Amanda.'

'What's this about?'

'I believe two of my colleagues were here earlier to discuss an incident at Roseneath Primary School.'

Alice sighed. 'If by incident you mean the poisoning of Mrs Kingston, then yes there were some questions asked and answered.'

Graves smiled slightly. 'We have some more questions.'

Amanda noticed a slight tightening around the mouth of young constable Wilson. It seemed he wasn't entirely comfortable with the brusque tone of his superior. Amanda stored that information away in case it came in handy later. Alice always told her that what wasn't said was sometimes as important as what was.

'Amanda, my name is Detective Graves from the Wellington CIB. Do you know what that is?'

Amanda shook her head.

'We deal with serious crimes,' Graves said. 'Like the poisoning of Mrs Kingston. And the latest incident. Do you know Helen Gregory?'

'Yes, she's in my class at school.'

'And how would you describe your relationship with her?'

'We get on alright.'

Graves gestured for Constable Wilson to hand him something. The constable reached into a small bag he was carrying and pulled out a book. When Graves turned it around Alice saw it was Amanda's school book. The words *I hate Helen*

Gregory were clearly written across the cover.

'Want to try again?'

Amanda shot a look at her grandmother who gave a tiny nod. She turned back to the policemen and shrugged.

'She's a pain in the butt.'

'This implies a stronger feeling than that,' Graves tapped the cover with is finger.

'I'm twelve. I hate things easily. I'm pretty sure I've written the same thing about half the people in my school, including the teachers, and even … my grandmother sometimes.'

Wilson flashed a grin before readopting his solemn expression. Graves scowled and tossed the book onto the coffee table. It slid across the surface and fell off the other side onto the ground. Amanda automatically picked it up and put it onto the couch next to her.

'Where were you at 3.30pm today?'

'She was at home,' Alice replied.

'Can anyone verify that?'

'You mean apart from me?'

Graves glared at her.

'You're her grandmother, in my experience family members don't provide the best alibis.'

Amanda saw Alice mentally take her gloves off.

'Was there a specific reason my granddaughter needs an alibi?'

'No, I just like coming into random strangers' houses and asking stupid questions.'

'What a quaint habit,' replied Alice.

'Now you listen here …'

'I find listening so hard these days. I'm afraid my mind isn't what it used to be. You were about to tell me what you thought

THIRTEEN

Amanda had done.'

Graves' cheeks were dark as he clenched his fists and Amanda wondered if Alice had misjudged the length of his fuse.

'This afternoon someone broke into the Gregory house and attacked Helen Gregory. She has a black eye and scratches on her arms and neck. Amanda's schoolbook was found outside the house,' Wilson said softly. He switched his steady gaze from Alice to Amanda.

'Did Helen say I attacked her?' Amanda asked incredulously.

'No, apparently the attacker wore a mask. Miss Gregory was too shaken to give us much of a description,' Graves said. He seemed to have recovered his temper.

'That poor girl. How unfortunate. Well, I completely understand you have to ask, but gentlemen, is it really your theory that Amanda became so overwhelmed with anger that she broke into her classmate's house, first stopping to don a disguise, attacked her, then paused outside the house to drop evidence that would point directly to her, before coming home for milk and cookies?'

'Milk and cookies?' Graves repeated.

'Metaphorically.'

'Our job is to look at the facts, and the fact is Amanda doesn't have an alibi. Blimmin' suspicious if you ask me.'

'Not really though, is it?' Alice replied. 'Most people don't have alibis. And most people don't live their lives thinking they need one. When Amanda is at school, I am home alone. If the police burst through my door, I've no one to back up my claim that I was in the shower when such and such happened. Where were you at 3.30 this afternoon, Detective?'

'I was doing some paperwork.'

'Can anyone verify that?'

Another fleeting smile crossed Wilson's face.

'Don't be ridiculous,' Graves said.

'When did you last see your schoolbook?' Wilson asked Amanda.

'I don't remember.'

'How convenient,' Graves interjected.

'It's my math book, and we didn't have math today. I thought that book was in my bag.'

'Where do you store your bag at school?' asked Alice.

Amanda looked at her grandmother curiously then replied, 'On a hook outside the classroom. All the bags get hung up together on the wall.'

'I see,' Alice said. 'So anyone could have taken it while you were in class.'

'I guess so.'

'That proves nothing!'

'You mistake my intention, Detective Graves. I'm not attempting to prove anything. I'm pointing out that there are a lot of unknowns that need to be considered before accusing my twelve-year-old granddaughter of assault.'

Detective Graves abruptly stood up. 'We'll be back.' He stormed out of the room leaving an apologetic Constable Wilson to mutter goodbye before following his superior out of the house.

Amanda got to her feet and started pacing.

'What's going on? Do they think I attacked Helen? I would never attack her. Why would I? She's totally not worth it.'

'Calm down,' Alice said mildly.

'Calm down! They're not going to handcuff you and throw you in jail.'

THIRTEEN

She paced for a while longer before flopping down in the chair previously occupied by Constable Wilson.

'Feel better?'

'No. Yes, I guess.'

Alice waited until Amanda sat up in her chair.

'Okay, so who would want to attack Helen and why are they trying to frame me?'

'Indeed,' replied Alice. 'And here's a third question. Was the assault on Helen related to the poisoning of Mrs Kingston?'

FOURTEEN

Wellington, August 2021

'What would she have worth stealing?'

Alice took a sip of tea and considered this. She was surprised Teresa didn't already know the answer.

'I've taken a cursory look around her apartment and nothing leapt out at me. But then I wouldn't know what might be worth taking.'

Teresa let out a half laugh as she looked at Alice with sparkling eyes.

'Oh of course, I forget how sheltered your life has been.'

'I was never a thief.'

'You've never told me what you were, but if half the rumours are true then I should be clutching my pearls just in case.'

Alice patted her friend on the arm. 'You're safe with me, Teresa. I would never do anything to hurt you.'

'For which I am eternally grateful.'

'But that's not to say I couldn't.'

Alice held up Teresa's watch and Teresa's eyes grew large as

FOURTEEN

she checked her empty wrist.

'I thought you said you weren't a thief ... I can see retirement has done nothing to dull your skills.'

'Thankfully.' Alice buckled the watch back onto Teresa's wrist and gave her another pat. 'Anyway when I visited her living room there were certainly some valuable items there, but ...'

'What is it?' Teresa asked. She placed her cup on the coffee table and looked at Alice expectantly.

'Well, like I said, I'm not a thief, so I don't know what they were after.'

Teresa looked disappointed, which confirmed to Alice that her friend had come for gossip rather than tea.

'I will tell you one thing I noticed. Her jewellery is authentic but inexpensive.'

Teresa clasped her hands together as if afraid Alice was going to reach over and pluck her wedding ring off her finger. 'Perhaps she keeps her valuable jewellery in a safe overnight. I never take mine off, well except for when I'm swimming. My husband put it on my finger forty years ago and that's where it will stay.'

'Admirable.'

'I have noticed you don't wear one. I presume at some point there was a Mr Atkinson. Oh wait, didn't you change your name a year or two back? What was it? Strong?'

Alice nodded. 'We didn't have much money for rings back then, so we decided not to bother. And after he died it didn't seem worth it.'

'I'm sorry. You never talk about him, but I shouldn't have pried.'

'It's fine. It happened so long ago there are no fresh emotions left, just old stale ones.'

'You never talk about your family either, apart from Amanda.'

'Amanda is my family.'

'Of course.' Teresa looked around the apartment. 'Is that a new pot plant?'

Alice rolled her eyes. 'Vanessa brought it. For some reason she believes having something to care for will stop me losing my marbles.'

'She actually said that?'

'Words to that effect.'

What Vanessa had actually said was something about plants being proven to enhance wellbeing and provide a sense of purpose through the care of them. She'd been spouting things like that since Alice had recently uncovered a box of papers that had belonged to her mother. It had been the first time she'd opened the box in decades and for some reason Vanessa seemed to believe it had evoked a feeling of melancholy. She seemed concerned that Alice was going to start shuffling around the apartment in her dressing gown and slippers, and no amount of reassurances or snapping, or pointing out that she didn't even own a dressing gown, were enough to reassure her.

'Brave woman,' Teresa said.

As if waiting for such an introduction, the front door opened and Vanessa walked in.

'We were just talking about you.'

'I'd say "all good, I hope", but knowing how hard it is to get a compliment out of Alice I'd guess not. Hi Teresa.'

'I compliment you – when you deserve it.'

Vanessa placed the bags she'd been carrying onto the kitchen bench.

FOURTEEN

'You realise how that sounds right?' she said.

'What have you got there?'

'I noticed you were out of some stuff, so I went shopping.'

Teresa laughed. 'How do I get a Vanessa? Come and work for me. I'll compliment you all the time.'

'Tempting,' Vanessa replied with a smile. 'But I think I'll stick with Alice for now.'

Teresa became serious. 'I was talking to Freda earlier, and she said she wasn't feeling safe at Silvermoon. With everything that has been happening over the last couple of years, she's trying to persuade Les to move.'

Alice frowned. 'She mentioned that to me as well. I didn't realise she was serious.'

'You know Freda, she'll be fine.'

'Are you feeling unsafe?' asked Alice.

'Not at all. As long as you're around, there's no need to feel worried. I'd better be off. Vanessa, let me know if you change your mind about that job.' Teresa stood up. 'Goodbye, Alice. Thank you for the tea.'

As the door swung closed behind Teresa, Alice went to the kitchen to peer into the paper bags Vanessa had brought.

'I thought you were doing research.'

'I was, I did, but then I got food as well.'

'I get food deliveries every week.'

'I know, but I was going past the supermarket anyway.'

'You shouldn't have.'

Vanessa gave her a puzzled look. 'What's the big deal?'

'I'm not training you to become a delivery person.'

'It's called being nice, Alice. And you see, nice people do things without being asked.'

'I know that!'

'And nice people buy you this.' Vanessa reached into the second bag and pulled out a bottle of whiskey.

'Why?'

'To restock some of the flasks you've got around the place. You thought I hadn't noticed?'

Alice had thought exactly that. Vanessa knew about some of the flasks she had hidden around the apartment, but Alice doubted she knew all of them. If she was completely honest with herself she wasn't sure she remembered the location of all of them either. Many of the flasks were empty, but some of the more easily accessible ones contained a sample of nicely aged alcohol. Every now and then she liked to retrieve one, think about where and when she'd got it, and take a tipple. In recent days, more now than then. She thought she'd been subtle about it, but apparently she was slipping. Or Vanessa was keeping a closer eye on her than she realised.

She took the bottle and examined the label. 'It's twenty-year-old special label.'

Vanessa shrugged. 'I asked for the best they had.'

Alice stared as Vanessa busied herself putting the shopping away.

'How did you pay for this?'

'That's impolite,' Vanessa replied.

Alice sighed. 'Thank you.' She carefully placed the bottle on the bench.

'Well, don't gush about it.'

'How many?'

'How many what?'

'Flasks.'

Vanessa paused with a can of chicken soup in her hand. 'Four.'

FOURTEEN

'Where?'

She put the can down and grinned. 'Cereal packet in the cupboard. Inside the book on the history of Scotland. Taped to the bottom of the coffee table. And there's one in that hideous remote control holder hanging off the side of the couch.'

'Very good.'

'How many did I miss?'

'More than you found. And the holder *is* hideous but it was a gift, and at least I always know where the television control is. Right, onto more important things. Talking to Teresa helped to clarify a few things in my mind about the attack on Sylvia.'

'Like what?'

'Like the fact that there were plenty of valuable things in her apartment in plain sight. Even if the attacker knew nothing about antiques, he would at least have taken the jewellery she was wearing.'

'Maybe none of her stuff looked that expensive?'

'You really do buy all your furniture at the discount store, don't you? Do you remember the glass figurine on her side table?'

'Yeah. It was a duck or chicken or something.'

'Chicken? Who would want a figurine of a chicken? Honestly, dear. It was a Lalique crystal swan and at a guess it's worth about six thousand dollars.'

'Holy—'

'No, but I think the white porcelain ornament in the shape of a book on her coffee table might be.'

'Okay. It's scary what you got from that five-minute visit.'

'As I've told you, dear, it's important to notice everything when you enter a room. You never know when what you see will be useful. In fact, I'm sure I've seen that porcelain book before. I just can't think where.'

'You mean you can't instantly recall that you saw it in Baron von Hammersmith the Third's villa in the south of France in the Fall of 1978?'

'Don't be ridiculous, dear. In 1978, I was with the prince.'

'You're joking.'

'Why would I joke about something like that?'

'What prince?'

'That's not important. Regarding the task you were given earlier, did you find out anything?'

'I did a search using the retirement village names and looked for any reported thefts, but nothing jumped out.'

'Hmm. How reliable is the internet thingie?'

'The internet thingie is not very reliable unless you're looking for recipes or cat videos. It's completely possible that there was something there that was overlooked by searching by the wrong words.'

'Then you used the wrong words.'

'Or there was nothing there to find.'

'There's one way to find out for sure.'

Vanessa sighed. 'You're sending me back to the computer, aren't you?'

'Count yourself lucky,' Alice replied with a grin. 'Before there were computers, we had to use other methods of finding things out.'

'Carrier pigeon? Smoke signals? Pony Express?'

'You realise I was born in 1922 and not 1822.'

'Is there a difference?'

'Cheeky, sod. I meant the telephone. We call some of these places and suggest I'm looking to move. But I couldn't possibly commit without knowing that I'm moving somewhere safe.'

FOURTEEN

'They won't tell you,' Vanessa replied. 'Not if it'll put you off moving in.'

'No, you're right. Management wouldn't tell me if the building was about to fall down and all the residents were barking mad. So I will ask to speak with one of the residents.'

'You think that'll work?'

'You've worked here long enough to know, dear, that we old people like a good story.'

FIFTEEN

Wellington, March 1994

Amanda stared at Marion. The girl had come running up to her that morning as soon as she'd walked through the front gates. Apparently in Helen's absence, it was acceptable to talk to Amanda, and Marion had been busting to talk about what happened to Helen.

Marion grabbed her by the arm and dragged her to a seat next to the playground.

'Helen was attacked! In her home! They say that she's in hospital and she might die!'

'Who's they?' asked Amanda.

'What? Oh, my mum was talking to Isabelle's mum who heard from Emilia's mum that Helen was badly hurt. They said she might lose her eye.'

'Really?'

'Yeah, it's so awful. Maybe she'll have to have a glass eye. Or maybe she'll wear an eyepatch like a pirate.'

Amanda quite liked the bubbly girl sitting next to her.

FIFTEEN

Marion was shorter than Amanda and vibrated with this nervous energy that threatened to judder her glasses right off her face. A few months ago, on Amanda's first day at school, Marion had raced up to her and declared them future best friends. Which is why it had hurt so much when Marion had let herself fall under Helen's rule.

'It's probably not that serious.'

Marion looked around to make sure they weren't being overheard, before leaning in and lowering her voice. 'Helen told me a secret. She said she was in danger.'

'What? When?'

Marion's face showed how much she loved knowing something important. 'Yesterday. She said she knew something and she was worried because she thought the person who poisoned Mrs Kingston would find out and get her.'

'Why didn't she tell the police?'

'I don't know,' Marion replied. She seemed dismayed to be missing vital information from the story.

'Did she say who she thought was coming after her?'

Marion shook her head. 'No, but I think … I think she thought it was someone she knew.'

Amanda frowned. First the police show up thinking she attacked Helen, now this. Had Helen really thought she was going to hurt her?

Before she could question Marion further the first bell rang and they had to go to class. Amanda mulled it all over while she was supposed to be doing a math problem.

'Amanda, can you tell us the answer to the first problem?'

'I don't know,' she muttered.

'Speak up, please,' the teacher said.

Amanda sat up straight and looked at the equation in front

of her. 'Fifty-three,' she said after a few seconds of furious thinking.

'Correct.' Thankfully the teacher didn't ask her to explain her workings because it had been a complete guess.

'Excuse me, Miss Boland.' Marion had her arm pointed straight at the ceiling.

'Yes, Marion.'

'I was wondering if it was true that Helen was horribly hurt by someone in her house?'

Miss Boland gave Marion a stern look. It was one that said this was a topic she wasn't prepared to talk about. 'Which question is that on your math work, Marion?'

Suitably cowed, Marion lowered her hand and her head at the same time.

Next to her Jenny Bailey put her own hand up and the teacher gestured for her to speak.

'The answer to question two is 70. I heard that Helen was attacked by someone at school.'

'Don't be ridiculous, Jenny, where did you hear that?'

Jenny shrugged. 'I don't know, everyone is saying it.'

'Well, I've heard enough. This is a classroom, not a place for spreading rumours.'

'I heard the police already know who did it.'

'Jenny! Enough!'

'Sorry, Miss Boland.'

Miss Boland turned to walk back to the front of the classroom and Jenny looked across at Amanda. She mouthed something. Amanda wasn't completely sure, but it looked like 'I know it was you'.

At lunch, it felt like the entire school was talking about Helen Gregory. If Helen had been there, she'd have been over the

FIFTEEN

moon about all the attention.

Marion caught Amanda's arm as they were leaving the classroom. She clearly wanted to continue their earlier discussion and Amanda was happy to listen. When she realised she had learned everything Marion knew, she made an excuse about using the toilet and escaped. By the time she was two steps away Marion had found someone else and was retelling the same story.

The closest toilets were inside the classroom block. Amanda didn't need to go but she locked herself into a stall for five minutes anyway, just to make sure Marion had properly moved on.

As she opened the door to leave the toilets, she heard voices in the hallway. She paused when she heard someone say Helen's name.

'Honestly, this used to be such a nice suburb, but with what happened to Frances, and now Helen ... The police have been at school more in the last two days than in the previous ten years.'

Amanda recognised Miss Boland's voice.

'I know,' came the reply. 'They were into my shed. Looking for poison they said. Took away some stuff I had for the rats.'

It sounded like Mr Harrison, the caretaker.

'Terrible. Surely they don't think you made her sick.'

'Who knows. Don't think they'd say until they slap me in cuffs.'

'Goodness. You've very calm about it.'

'Why should I worry? Maybe it was my poison, maybe it wasn't. But it wasn't me that put it in her cuppa.'

'I believe you. If anyone has a motive, it's Glynis. She and Frances had a big disagreement last week.'

There was a clatter followed by the sound of running feet.

'Selwyn! What have you been told about running inside?'

Amanda slipped through the door into the hallway in time to see Miss Boland and Mr Harrison disappear around the corner at the far end.

She needed to talk to Alice but she wouldn't get the chance until later that afternoon.

After school, Amanda had netball practice. She didn't particularly like netball, but she was naturally athletic and if she'd put her mind to it she might have been the best player on the team. The problem was that it was a team sport. And Alice had taught her that relying on others was setting yourself up to fail. The only reason Amanda played was that Alice had insisted. Lesson two – in any environment, gathering information is key, and the best way to get information at school was to join a team.

Today, there was just as much gossip as balls flying between players. Amanda tried to keep her mouth shut.

'Come on, Mandy,' Jenny said, throwing the ball to her in a chest pass. 'You must know something. Especially about Helen.'

Amanda gritted her teeth. Someone calling her Mandy was the same as her calling Alice Gran. She resisted the urge to fire the ball at Jenny's head.

'Why would I know anything about Helen?' she replied. 'I don't even like her.'

'Exactly,' Jenny said triumphantly. 'I bet it was you who attacked her.'

'Why would I do that?'

'I don't know, maybe you're jealous of how cool she is.'

'She's not cool. Although she does have some cool stuff,'

FIFTEEN

Amanda admitted.

'I think you want to be like her.'

'That's stupid.'

'You're stupid.'

Amanda passed the ball back to Jenny, a little too hard, and right at her face. Jenny ducked just in time.

'Amanda,' the coach yelled. 'Be more careful.'

'Sorry,' Amanda replied sweetly.

Jenny ran over and picked up the ball. Amanda waited for her to throw it back, but instead Jenny joined another group, leaving Amanda standing by herself. She covered her embarrassment by crouching down to tie her shoelaces. When she stood up the coach called the team together and they spent the rest of the practice going over positions and game play.

After practice, Amanda picked up her schoolbag and walked to the front gate. She glanced over her shoulder and saw Jenny and three of the other girls were looking in her direction.

Whatever. Who needs them?

SIXTEEN

Wellington, August 2021

Alice watched the uniformed officers carefully search the grass under the trees by the entrance to Silvermoon. They were methodical and careful, and they were looking on the wrong side of the driveway. Someone had obviously read the surveillance video wrong.

She thought briefly about popping down to tell them they were looking in the wrong spot. She watched a moment longer, then went back to her phone calls.

So far she'd spoken with residents of two of Sylvia Gregory's previous retirement homes. The first had spent ten minutes talking about her cat before Alice could end the conversation. The second had thought that Syliva was the best human being walking the planet and had been completely devastated when she'd moved. But she couldn't recall any thefts occurring around the same time.

Alice dialled the number for Garden City Retirement Village in Christchurch. The name made her imagine old people

SIXTEEN

growing tomatoes. She grinned when she wondered what picture people had of the Silvermoon Retirement Village.

She got past the receptionist and was put through to the manager, who passed her on to the resident wellness liaison (whatever that was) and finally she found herself connected with a woman called Beth.

'Of course, I remember Sylvia. Great golf player. It was a shame she moved away. She never gave me a chance to win my money back.'

'What money was that?'

'Oh, not high stakes. We used to wager on the game, a dollar per hole. She was a one. The last time we played I lost ninety dollars.'

'Beth, math isn't my strongest skill but that is more than a dollar per hole.'

Beth laughed. 'We decided as a one-off to raise the stakes to five dollars. And of course I had a terrible round and lost every hole. Then she moved away the next week. I didn't even know she was leaving until her granddaughter arrived.'

'You met Helen?'

'I did.' Her tone suggested it wasn't a pleasant encounter.

'I did too,' Alice continued. 'An interesting woman.'

Beth snorted. 'As interesting as a huntsman spider in your letterbox.'

'You're Australian?'

'I spent (or misspent) my youth over there. Anyway, I only met Helen twice, once when she was moving Sylvia in and the other when she moved her out.'

'How long did Sylvia live there?'

'Oh, not long. About four months, if I recall correctly.'

'Did anything unusual happen while she was there?'

'Like what?'

'I don't know,' Alice said. 'Anything. To Sylvia or to anyone she knew?'

'I suppose you're talking about the mugging. You could just have asked me directly. No need to pussyfoot about.'

Alice sat up straighter. 'What mugging?' she repeated.

'Well, it was hardly a mugging. Sylvia wasn't hurt and he didn't get any of her valuables. She was walking along one of the paths next to the village early one morning and a thug on a skateboard knocked her down.'

So Sylvia had been attacked at a previous residence as well. Coincidence?

They chatted for a few moments longer, then Alice pretended there was someone at the door and excused herself.

Now that she knew a little more, she thought she'd pay another visit to Sylvia. Looking at her watch, she realised it was close to lunchtime. She'd eat first and then go for a walk.

Thanks to Vanessa, her pantry and fridge were fully stocked but as Alice perused the options nothing took her fancy. Her appetite was hit and miss these days. She ate at mealtimes because it was expected. If she missed the occasional meal then it wasn't going to hurt. She closed the fridge and retrieved a flask from the Muesli box in the cupboard. It amused her to hide something so tasty inside a box of food she found so unpalatable. This one was black with an M stamped into the bottom. She ran her finger over the letter as she remembered the rather unpleasant gentleman from whom she had obtained this particular flask, in 1972. She had acquired this souvenir at the same time as she had liberated a small gold bell with diamonds set in the handle.

SIXTEEN

Alice frowned. She'd always said she wasn't a thief, but the object in her hand suggested otherwise. She shook off the thought. While technically she had stolen the hip flasks, none of them were particularly valuable. She kept them purely as mementos of her past adventures.

She unscrewed the cap and took a sip, savouring the smooth whisky before reluctantly doing the lid back up. Once she'd replaced the flask in its hiding spot, she made herself a piece of toast.

She was brushing away the crumbs, when Vanessa came in. 'Something is going on.'

Alice raised her eyebrows. 'Something is always going on somewhere, dear, please try and be more specific.'

'I just saw two police officers and Tracey hurrying around the corner out front.'

Alice checked the window. Sure enough, the officers that had been searching the driveway were gone.

'Go find out,' she said.

Vanessa disappeared out the door and a few minutes later Alice saw her leave the building and stride in the direction of the Olympic complex. Minutes passed while Alice waited for her to reappear. She went to the bedroom and collected her binoculars from beneath the window. Peering through them, everything blurred then sharpened as she fiddled with the dial. She turned to the right and saw Les and Freda seated at an outside table at Charlie's. They were both looking at the apartment building. Alice turned the binoculars back towards the driveway. She caught a glimpse of a dark coloured car in the visitor car park between the café and Olympic complex. It was tucked between a van and the dumpster, so she could only see part of the front.

Thoughtfully she put the binoculars down. It could have been the same car Helen had driven the previous day but it was hard to tell at this angle.

Impatiently she waited for Vanessa to return. Alice was tapping her foot and scowling when she finally came through the door.

'Sylvia is missing.'

Alice stopped tapping. 'What do you mean *missing*?'

Vanessa walked to the window. 'How many ways could I mean? She's missing. Gone. Vanished. Abducted by aliens. Disappeared off the face of the Earth. No one knows where she is.'

'Vanessa!'

'Alright,' Vanessa said with a laugh, leaning back against the window, her hands in her pockets. 'She was supposed to be having lunch with Helen. But when Helen got to her apartment Sylvia wasn't there. Apparently she doesn't drive and no one remembers seeing her leave, but she isn't there.'

'They checked inside her apartment?'

'Yeah. Helen had keys. She did a quick search then went and got Tracey who took the police in with her. They're doing a door-to-door search now.'

Alice shook her head slowly. 'It seems like an overreaction. How do they know she hasn't just gone for a walk? Or perhaps she's having a swim in the pool? Or maybe she's in the games room?'

'I don't know. Helen seemed worried.'

'What sort of worried?'

'There's more than one sort?'

'Of course. Worried about being late for a hair appointment is quite different from being worried about a missing relative.'

SIXTEEN

'Good point.'

'Why thank you,' Alice responded.

'Then I guess she was super worried, almost panicked. She kept checking her watch, like she was late for something.'

Alice glanced at her own watch. It was a little after twelve. She tried to recall whether Teresa had mentioned seeing Sylvia that morning.

'Someone must have seen her,' she said to herself.

'I'm sure she'll show up,' Vanessa replied. 'People don't just disappear.'

'Rubbish. People disappear all the time. But we don't yet know if she's disappeared or just can't be found.'

'Then I guess we'll find out.'

Alice didn't reply. Instead she picked up the television remote control and threw it at Vanessa.

Vanessa tried to duck, smacked her head on the window pane but managed to get one hand out of a pocket in time to deflect the remote from her face.

'Ow! What the actual heck!' She rubbed the back of her head and gaped at Alice in shock.

'If your hands weren't so far down in your pockets they were touching your knees then you would have caught it. If you insist on using your pockets for something other than a place to store things then make sure you keep one hand free. You never know when something is going to be thrown at you.'

'I thought this was a safe place.'

'It is. I wasn't trying to hurt you.'

'Yet I'm hurt.'

'Which you wouldn't be if you didn't have your hands in your pockets.'

'You could've just told me,' Vanessa grumbled as she walked

over to the kitchen. 'What do you want for lunch.'
'I had a slice of toast.'
'Toast is not lunch, it's breakfast. You need more than that.'
'I'm not hungry.'
'What about eggs?'
'I said I'm not hungry.'
'I could do an omelette.'
'Dear, stop fussing, I said I'm not hungry.'
Vanessa paused with her hand on the fridge door handle. 'Well I'm hungry. I'll make extra just in case.'
Alice glared, but Vanessa smiled benignly in a way that reminded Alice of herself. It only added to her annoyance.
When the smell of the omelette wafted across to her Alice had to admit that it smelled pretty good. She made a show of grudgingly accepting the plate when it was offered, then promptly ate it all.
'I got a call from Mum this morning,' Vanessa said.
'Oh?'
Vanessa put her plate on the coffee table and tucked her legs under her. Alice waited for her to continue. 'Mum and I had a fight just before I came to work here. She thought I was wasting my life. I told her to butt out. It got pretty heated.'
Alice remembered her often fractious relationship with her own mother. Heated was a polite term for some of their conversations.
'We didn't talk, haven't talked, since then. Like, I wanted to reach out, but some of the things I said ... some of the things she said ... I wasn't sure if I'd be apologising or restarting the fight.'
'And you were embarrassed,' Alice said.
'So, so embarrassed. I'm usually a pretty relaxed person –

SIXTEEN

you know, when things aren't being thrown at me. But she rubs me the wrong way every time.'

'Because you're similar.'

'What? No. I'm nothing like my mother.'

'I said the same thing. I was lying to myself too.'

'I'm not—'

A quiet knock at the door interrupted her. Vanessa opened it to reveal Sylvia Gregory, looking extremely agitated.

'Can I come in?'

'Of course,' Alice called from the couch.

Sylvia waited for the door to close behind her before she spoke again. 'I ... oh dear. I should go.'

'But you only just got here,' Alice replied with a smile.

'Do you realise that your granddaughter is looking for you?' said Vanessa.

That seemed to upset Sylvia more. She began pacing the floor, wringing her hands together. 'Oh dear, oh dear. It's just ... I know she's going to be angry. But I can't ... I don't want to ...'

'Perhaps a cup of tea?' Alice suggested. 'Or something stronger?'

Sylvia stopped pacing, her eyes lit up at the offer of something to drink.

Just then they all heard the muffled sound of activity outside. Vanessa checked out the window.

'It's the search party.'

She opened a window and they clearly heard voices calling for Sylvia.

Vanessa and Alice turned just in time to see Sylvia reaching for the door.

'Wait,' called Alice.

Antiques and Assault

'No, I shouldn't have come. She'll be angry. I must ... oh dear.' Sylvia quickly left the apartment.

'What was that all about?' Vanessa finally said.

'I have no idea. Why did you let her leave? What's happening outside?'

Vanessa turned back to the window.

'She's just come out the front door. The police are rushing up to her. I can't hear exactly what they're saying but Tracey put her arm around her. Now they're all walking back towards Sylvia's apartment.'

Vanessa watched a little while longer, then closed the window.

'That was weird, right? I mean, it wasn't just me, that was really weird.'

'It was certainly strange.'

'Come on, you can say it. It was weird.'

SEVENTEEN

Wellington, March 1994

'It's super weird.'

Alice grimaced. 'Please do not use that word, Amanda. Situations might be unusual or strange but they are never weird.'

'But it *is* weird,' Amanda insisted. 'I didn't do anything but the whole school is going around like I beat up Helen and tried to kill Mrs Kingston.'

'Which is a sad reflection of the gullibility of society, but most definitely not weird.'

'Huh?'

Alice picked up an object off the table and passed it to Amanda who sighed and held it up to the light. Amanda breathed on it and studied the object for a moment before handing it back.

'Crystal.'

'How can you tell?'

'When I breathed on it the surface clouded but it cleared

straight away. If it was glass it would have stayed cloudy longer.'

'Exactly, well done.'

'What did you mean it's a reflection of society?'

Alice picked up a different item and handed it to Amanda before replying.

'One person can be persuaded to see your point of view, or not, depending on how strong their convictions are.'

'Huh? Fake.'

'Why?'

Amanda picked the small lump of gold out of the glass of water. 'Real gold is heavy and sinks. This floated.'

'Correct. A single person will stick to their beliefs as long as possible. But if you put them into a room filled with people that are saying something different, most people will eventually be persuaded that their view is wrong. I doubt many students think you're guilty, but enough are saying it that the others don't want to go against the rest. Understand?'

Amanda scrunched up her face like she'd just eaten an ice cream and had brain freeze. 'I think so. You're saying if enough people shout fire then everyone will believe there's a fire even when there isn't one.'

'Precisely.'

'How do I stop them thinking there's a fire?'

'You redirect their attention.'

Alice held up a small green dragon figurine. Amanda took it from her and examined it.

'You're saying I need to accuse someone else.'

'No, dear, I'm saying find out who actually did it.'

'Fake,' Amanda said. It slipped from her hand, hit the corner of the coffee table and fell to the floor in two pieces.

SEVENTEEN

'Oops sorry.' She picked the pieces up and froze when she saw the expression on Alice's face. 'It was fake, wasn't it?'

Alice took the broken figure from her. 'Let's just say if I asked you to pay it off it would take … a hundred and ninety-two years of pocket money.

Amanda's eyes grew so wide Alice thought one might pop out of her head. 'I … I'm sorry.'

'Never mind, dear.'

'I don't want to go to school anymore. Can't I go back to my old school?'

'We talked about that.'

Amanda sat up excitedly. 'Why can't you teach me at home? You know everything, I don't need that place.'

Alice shook her head. 'Much as it pains me to admit, there are some things I can't teach you.'

'Then I don't need to learn them.'

'Amanda.' Alice leaned over and took her hand. 'Socialising, being able to interact with people. I can't teach you that. You need to go to school. You need to be with people your own age.'

Amanda slumped in her chair with a miserable look on her face.

'This won't do,' Alice said. 'Up.'

'What?'

'Get up.'

Reluctantly Amanda stood.

'Change into your gi and meet me by the front door.'

'Gran!'

'I'm going to make a call. Off you go.'

Thirty minutes later they climbed the stairs to a small martial arts studio on the edge of the city. The black belt instructor stood in the middle of the mat waiting for them. He beckoned to Amanda. She walked onto the mat and looked at Alice.

'I don't want to do this now.'

The instructor, a solidly build man with long brown hair in a ponytail, bowed to Amanda. Reluctantly she bowed back. As the two took fighting stances, Alice began circling the mat.

The instructor threw a punch and Amanda easily blocked it. He followed up with a low front kick which she also blocked.

'Question, is Mrs Kingston's poisoning and Helen's attack linked?'

Amanda ducked under the next punch and threw one of her own which was blocked. 'Really? We're doing this now?'

She flicked her eyes to Alice and the instructor took the opportunity to sweep her legs from under her.

Amanda collapsed to the ground and glared at Alice. 'Look what you made me do!'

'I never told you to look at me.'

Amanda sprang to her feet and took guard. The instructor attacked with a series of punches and kicks, all of which Amanda evaded or blocked.

'Yes,' Amanda panted. 'They are linked. They have to be.'

'Why?'

'Because …' Amanda ducked under a punch and threw one of her own, connecting with the instructor's ribs. He barely reacted, other than backing away and smiling slightly. '… because it's unlikely that two things like this would happen right after each other.'

Alice nodded approvingly. 'And what do the two things have in common?'

The instructor closed with Amanda and tried to sweep her

SEVENTEEN

front leg again. She jumped, kicking out and catching him in the shoulder. He staggered back and Amanda dropped her guard and turned to Alice.

'Me. I'm the thing in common. I had a run-in with Mrs Kingston when she accused me of stealing, and my math book was found at Helen's house.'

Alice removed her shoes and bowed before stepping onto the mat. She walked up to Amanda and patted her on the arm.

'You're missing the more obvious connection.'

Amanda shook her head in frustration. Before Alice could go on, the instructor launched himself at the two of them. Alice pushed Amanda away and stepped back, letting the man go past. He swung an arm at her head and Alice leaned back so it missed, then grabbed it, pulled the man towards her, stuck her hip out and threw the man over and down to the mat.

'Whoa,' Amanda said.

She offered her hand to the instructor who declined it, climbing to his feet.

'How did you know?' he asked.

'You pulled your punch,' replied Alice.

'And ended up on my butt.'

'This time.'

The man bowed, then grinned. 'I'll get you next time, old woman.'

'One day, Ethan, one day.'

'Nice work, Amanda.' Ethan bowed to her then disappeared through a door marked 'Changing Room'.

'Who accused you of stealing?' Alice asked Amanda. 'Helen.'

'Yes. Helen accused you of stealing, and although she hasn't named you as her attacker, someone planted your book to ensure you would be suspected.'

'You think Helen did that? But why? Why would she hate me that much? I barely know her.'

'Perhaps it's time we approach this as a job. And what is the first thing we do when starting a job?'

'Find out about the mark.'

'Client, dear. Mark sounds crass.'

'Isn't a client someone who is paying you to do something for them?'

'Yes, which is precisely what we do, though they don't always know it.'

Amanda retrieved her bottle of water from the bag on the side of the mat and took a long drink.

'Okay,' she said. 'So let's find out more about Helen.'

Alice looked at her granddaughter's determined expression, so different from the defeated one earlier, and allowed herself a small smile.

EIGHTEEN

Wellington, August 2021

Alice slowly opened her eyes just as Vanessa shook her arm again.

'What? Stop pawing me like a drunken sailor.'

'I don't even know what to do with that.'

Alice sat up, realising she must have fallen asleep on the couch while watching television. She was wearing yesterday's clothes and the pale morning sun was competing with the overhead lights to illuminate the room.

'Are you okay?' asked Vanessa.

'Of course, I am. Have you never slept on the couch?'

'Oh sure, but usually there was alcohol involved. That's not important. The police are back at Sylvia's.'

'Another attack?'

'Something worse. There's an ambulance as well, but no one looks like they're in a hurry.'

Alice stretched and felt a pop in the middle of her back as a knot gave way.

'I'm a little sore from the couch. Perhaps a walk will help ease the kinks out.'

'What a good idea,' Vanessa replied.

Although Alice had said it lightly, it did take a few shuffling steps before the blood flowed into her feet and an elevator ride before her back and neck stopped aching. She disliked how Vanessa hovered next to her, arm poised to grab her in case she fell. Once they were safely down the front steps she picked up the pace and briskly walked the length of the building.

At the corner, she saw the ambulance and a police car parked outside Sylvia's apartment door. No one was visible.

'What shall we do?' asked Vanessa.

'Be concerned neighbours.'

Alice marched up to the apartment door and knocked loudly. It was immediately opened by a uniformed police officer.

'Hello, officer. We saw the ambulance and just wanted to check that our friend Sylvia is alright.'

'I'm sorry, ma'am. I can't let you in at the moment.'

'Oh dear. She was attacked recently. You're not saying that person came back, are you?'

'Ma'am, I'm going to have to ask you to return to your residence.'

A voice from inside the apartment said something and the officer turned to reply, giving Alice a view of the living room. Two paramedics stood in the middle of the room talking quietly. At their feet, partially obscured by the couch, lay Sylvia.

The officer turned back to Alice and held up his hands as if he was going to push her away. 'Please, ma'am. Return to your residence.'

Alice smiled. 'Of course. Please let me know if there's

EIGHTEEN

anything I can do to help poor Sylvia though. I'm Alice, just ask at reception for me, dear.'

Once they were safely away Vanessa asked, 'What did you see? That tree trunk of a cop was in my way.'

'Two paramedics standing idly while Sylvia lay on the floor. What does that tell you?'

Vanessa didn't need long to put it together. 'That she's dead.'

'Precisely.'

'Oh no. She's dead?'

'Not quite so loudly, dear. I'm sure the news will get around soon but there are more efficient ways than to be a town cryer.'

'No one is going to want to live here.'

'Don't exaggerate.'

'You're right, sorry. Apart from you, no one will want to live here.'

'Then we'll have to solve this as quickly as possible so people feel safe again.'

'Solve what? We don't even know what happened.'

'But we will. If Sylvia was killed, they will want to talk to people who knew her, and since I just made it clear to the officer that I knew her and where to find me, I'm going to guess we'll have a visit before morning tea.'

Alice was wrong. The knock on the door came thirty minutes later just as they were finishing breakfast.

Vanessa showed two police officers into the apartment and asked them to take a seat while Alice emptied her cup and went over to lean against the window sill. The policemen had to twist slightly in their seats to talk to her.

'I'm Sergeant Thomas and this is Constable Graves.'

Alice looked carefully at the young woman sitting with

pencil poised above notebook and said, 'Graves. Not a common name.'

'No ma'am.'

'New on the job?'

'Yes ma'am.'

'And no doubt been told to let the sergeant here do all the talking?'

Graves snuck a sideways look at her superior and gave a small smile.

'I've been trying to convince Vanessa here to take up a proper profession. What attracted you to police work?'

'Family, ma'am. My father was a detective.'

'If I could interrupt,' Thomas said. 'We are here because I'm sorry to inform you that Sylvia Gregory has died.'

'Murdered,' Alice said.

'What makes you say that?' Thomas sat forward in his chair with an eager expression.

'You wouldn't have come straight here if she'd had a heart attack,' Alice replied calmly.

'Still, why go straight to murder?'

Alice saw Graves write something down. 'A guess. No one seemed in a terrible hurry at her apartment this morning.'

'Are you sure you didn't go by there earlier?'

The sun exited from behind a cloud and bright light bathed the officers' faces, making them squint.

'How long have you been a sergeant, Sergeant?'

Thomas seemed taken aback by the change in conversation. 'Four years. Why?'

'I'm just nosy. Vanessa woke me up shortly before we saw you at Sylvia Gregory's apartment.'

'Is it your habit to go for a walk so soon after waking up?'

EIGHTEEN

'Well,' Alice chuckled, 'to be honest, I fell asleep on the couch last night so I thought a walk might help get the blood flowing. You know, circulation is an issue for the elderly, sergeant.'

'Can anyone verify your alibi?'

'I suppose it's possible that we are lying, but then that depends whether you think I killed Sylvia.'

'We're just trying to establish where everyone was first thing this morning.'

'That's the funny thing about alibis. Most people don't have one because most people don't realise they're going to need one. Come to think of it, where were you early this morning, Detective?'

'Sergeant ma'am. And I was at home.'

'Can anyone verify that?'

Another fleeting smile crossed Grave's face. Thomas frowned and settled back in his seat.

'Let's start again, shall we? How well did you know Sylvia Gregory?'

Feeling like she'd established her position in the conversation, Alice went to sit on the couch.

'Barely at all. We met for the first time a few days ago when she moved in.'

'Yet you were concerned enough to knock on her door this morning.'

'I saw the ambulance. It's called basic human compassion, Sergeant.'

Thomas looked mildly ashamed.

'I knew she had been attacked the other day. She stopped by to see me briefly yesterday, and that was the extent of our relationship.'

'What did she come and see you about?'

'Oh she wanted to thank me for checking on her after that terrible assault. Have you caught the man who did it?'

'That's not … I'm not able to comment on an open investigation.'

'Can you tell me how Sylvia was killed?'

'Enquiries are ongoing,' Thomas replied.

Vanessa came to sit next to Alice. 'Can you at least tell us if Alice is likely to be knifed in her sleep?'

'I don't believe you have anything to worry about in that regard,' Graves said with a smile.

'I told you I thought I saw a gun,' Alice said to Vanessa.

'It can't have been a gun or someone would have heard the shots,' replied Vanessa.

'What if they used one of those … what do you call them, silencing thingees?'

'I've read they don't really silence a gunshot, they just muffle it a little so someone would have still heard—'

'Ladies!' Thomas said. 'It wasn't a gun, or a knife. Now can we get back to my questions.'

There were only a couple more from the clearly annoyed police officer, before Vanessa showed him to the door.

'Very good, dear,' Alice said.

'Thanks. It's so easy to get information out of people if they don't know you're asking.'

'And now we know two things we didn't before. Sylvia Gregory was murdered.'

'And it wasn't a knife or a gun,' Vanessa concluded. 'Still leaves a considerable range of ways to kill someone though.'

'One step at a time, dear.'

'Okay, next step?'

Alice considered while staring out the window. It looked

EIGHTEEN

like it was going to be a good day. Not for Sylvia obviously, but weather-wise.

'I'd love to get into her apartment.'

'The police won't release it for days.'

'Oh, I don't think we need to wait quite that long. In the meantime, let's find out when Sylvia was last seen alive. And check the front gate camera to see if anyone came on to the property in the middle of the night.'

'I guess someone will have told Helen?'

'I would think Tracey will have taken care of that. Let's keep an eye out for her, I want to talk to her.'

'She'll be devastated.'

'Mmm, quite possibly. I think I'll wander down to gossip central while you check the camera footage.'

Vanessa screwed up her face. 'Gee, thanks.'

Alice accompanied her to the ground floor where they split up. The day had barely heated up thanks to a brisk southerly wind. Most of its effects were dispersed by the bordering trees and fence, but enough remained to send a chill through Alice as she walked.

Soon I'll look like a damn polar bear with all these extra layers.

Gossip central was an apt description for Charlie's. There was nothing like the combination of food, coffee, and open plan seating to get tongues wagging. Over the years Alice had gleaned plenty of useful information there, usually from an adjacent table.

Today the place was buzzing. After no thought at all she decided to skip the spinach, alfalfa, and kumara muffins. Next to the tray of muffins was a small box with a slit cut into the lid. It was here that residents could put their suggestions for muffin flavours. The café drew a suggestion out every couple of days and make it, no matter how unusual the suggestion. As a result, some of the muffins were truly delicious while others were borderline dangerous.

She paid for her coffee and turned to see Owen waving to her from a table in the corner.

'Don't tell me you're here for the same reason as the rest of them,' Owen said with a smile.

'Coffee and company?' Alice replied.

'You hate company, and you don't normally drink coffee this early.'

'I don't hate company! And I'll have you know I used to sip coffee every morning as the sun came up over the Pacific Ocean.'

'When did you live in America?' Owen said with barely concealed interest.

'What's going on there?' Alice gestured to where two police cars were now parked. The ambulance was gone.

'I think you already know,' said Owen.

'Perhaps, but indulge me.'

'It appears that our newest residence is also our most recently deceased.'

'Careful, Owen, that was almost a joke.'

'I would never jest about the departed.'

Alice studied her immaculately dressed friend and nodded. 'What happened to her?'

'Again, I suspect you know better than I.'

Alice assumed an innocent expression and Owen sighed.

'The current theory is the burglar from the other night came back and killed her.'

That was possible, most likely even, and was the theory that Alice was sure the police would latch onto. But she wasn't so

EIGHTEEN

sure. There was something bugging her.

Alice's drink was delivered to the table and she smiled and said thank you before turning back to her friend.

'Anyone saying they saw anything?'

'The only thing people saw were the ambulance and police car arriving.'

'I wonder who found her?' Alice said.

'Ah, there I can help you. It was Trudy.'

Owen pointed to the rear of the café where a young woman wearing a green groundskeeping staff uniform sat nursing a cup of coffee between both hands.

'You don't say. I'll be right back.'

Owen reached over and placed his hand on hers. 'You're not investigating this, are you?'

'Would that be a bad thing? I've got a pretty good track record around here.'

'Yes, and you've taken some terrible risks. You're not invulnerable, Alice, despite what you might think.'

'That's sweet, Owen dear, but I think crossing the café floor is safe enough.'

As she walked away, she struggled to stifle her irritation. Owen meant well, but he was one of those gentlemen-types who thought they had to protect the weaker women. Alice had used this to her advantage in allowing her to manipulate men many times over the years, but she still found it annoying.

'Hello Trudy.'

'Hi,' Trudy replied in a miserable voice.

Alice sat down in the opposite chair. She hadn't often spoken to the young woman since Trudy had started working at Silvermoon three months ago, just a wave or good morning, but Alice liked her. Trudy always had a big smile on her face.

Except for today.

'I understand you've had a big shock,' Alice said gently. 'Why haven't you gone home?'

Trudy fiddled nervously with her watch strap. 'The police said they might have some more questions, and honestly all my flatmates are at work or Uni and I don't want to be alone. I can tell you something for nothing Mrs Atkinson, seeing a dead body is not the same as seeing a dead bird.'

Alice had seen both and agreed with her.

'And you'd be surprised how many dead birds I've found around here in the bushes or on the lawn. Sometimes I think there must be a pack of wild cats living on the property.'

'No, just the one,' Alice muttered. 'Tell me what happened this morning.'

Trudy peered at her, the light from the food display reflecting of the small stud in the side of her nose. 'I've heard about you.'

'Oh?'

'They say you're good at investigating.'

'Is that what they say?'

Trudy grinned. 'Words to that effect.'

Alice returned her grin. 'I can imagine.'

'The police told me not to talk to anyone about what I saw.'

'Very sensible,' Alice replied.

Trudy snorted, then leaned in closer. 'I usually get here early, just to do a walk around. Like I said, I've been finding dead birds lying around the place and Tracey likes me to try and dispose of them before too many residents are up. Like old people have never seen a dead animal before.'

Alice nodded. 'I agree with you. Please, continue.'

'I did the rounds, picked up two dead birds, and rounded the corner to complete the loop when I saw the door to Mrs

EIGHTEEN

Gregory's apartment was open a little bit.'

'What time was this?'

'Six fifty-five.'

She looked at her watch as if it had stopped at that time.

'That's very precise.'

'I remember checking the time because I don't usually see anyone else until after seven. So I went over and knocked. There was no reply, so I peeked inside and called out.'

'And that's when you saw the body.'

'I figured maybe she'd fallen. I went in to see if I could help. And that's when I saw that she was … that her head had …'

'She'd been hit in the head?' Alice said.

Trudy nodded. 'She had blood on the side of her face and I checked her pulse, and there wasn't one.'

She looked like she was going to cry and Alice wished she had one of her flasks with her. The girl needed something stronger than coffee.

'What was she wearing?'

She thought she knew the answer already from her partial glimpse through the apartment door but wanted to give Trudy something to think about other than a bloodied face.

'A blue tracksuit, top and bottom, and she had running shoes on her feet.'

Where else would she have them? Alice decided now was not the time to point out the obvious.

'Anything else you remember seeing?'

Trudy shook her head. 'Are you going to catch the person who did this?'

'Do you not have faith in the police?'

'Like I said, I've heard about you,' Trudy replied. 'If it's between that lot and you, my money is on you.'

She looked towards the front door and something in her expression made Alice turn. Constable Graves stood just inside the door. When she saw Trudy, she made her way to the table.

'Then best I solve it. I'd hate for you to lose your money,' Alice said before standing up. 'Constable.'

'Ma'am.'

Alice returned to her seat at Owen's table.

'How is the poor girl?' he asked. Despite his reserved manner and officious dress sense, Owen had a heart of gold.

'She'll be fine.'

'And did your interrogation go well?'

'Please,' Alice replied, taking a sip of her lukewarm coffee. 'It barely qualified as an interview.'

'Learn anything useful?'

Alice smiled. 'I come here to get the gossip, not provide it to all the neighbouring tables.'

'Very well. Do try and stay safe, won't you?'

'Always do.'

NINETEEN

Wellington, March 1994

'Are you sure I'm the right person?'

Amanda nodded, innocence firmly displayed on her face.

'Alright,' Mrs Ferris sighed. 'Though I don't understand why your teacher thought this was a good idea.'

It hadn't taken much nudging to get her teacher to agree that Mrs Ferris was the perfect example of a highly skilled worker and an ideal choice for a project on the modern workforce. Most of her class were interviewing firefighters or police officers. Amanda's recent experience with the police had been enough for her and she didn't want to spend any more time with them. Besides, the project gave her the perfect opportunity to hang out in the office … where the student records were kept.

'I wanted to do something different from the rest of my class, and the other day when I was here I thought that you seemed like you knew everything that went on at the school and that's so amazing when there's so many students.'

Amanda heard Alice's voice in her head telling her she was babbling. She clamped her mouth shut and smiled.

'Well, thank you, Amanda. Sometimes I think no one realises that.' Mrs Ferris was typing on the computer as she spoke. 'My job is so much more than answering phones—'

The phone rang.

'Roseneath Primary School, Mrs Ferris speaking. Yes, that's fine, Mr Rogers, I'll let her teacher know.'

She hung up the phone and scribbled something on a piece of paper.

'Answering the phones is an important part of it too, of course, but there is so much more than that. I take care of deliveries, make payments, ensure the principal gets to her meetings on time.'

'Wow, sounds busy,' Amanda said. *And boring*.

'It can be quite challenging,' Mrs Ferris replied.

At that moment a boy burst into the office and excitedly announced that there was a fire in the boys' toilets.

'Rubbish!' Mrs Ferris said. 'What have I told you about telling fibs, Selwyn Johnson?'

Nevertheless, she sprang from her desk and rushed out of the room, followed by the breathless boy.

As soon as they were gone, Amanda ran around the desk to examine Mrs Ferris' computer. She hoped it was as easy to operate as Mrs Ferris made it look. She wiggled the mouse and the screen came to life. It might as well have been in a different language. Scanning the office she spotted the filing cabinets and quickly opened the one marked A-H. Finding Helen's file she scanned it as quickly as she could, knowing that the small paper fire she'd suggested Selwyn Johnson 'would never be brave enough to start' in the boys' toilets wouldn't keep Mrs

NINETEEN

Ferris distracted for long.

She checked the clock above the door. It'd been two minutes but it felt like twenty. Suddenly the sound of footsteps approached the office door. Amanda quicky closed the cabinet drawer and reached out to pick up the phone receiver, just as the office door opened and Mrs Ferris entered.

'Amanda, what are you doing?'

Amanda put the phone down. 'The phone rang and I wasn't sure what to do, so answered it. But they hung up. I'm sorry, I thought I was helping.'

She stood up and backed away from the desk.

Mrs Ferris's stern expression softened. 'Thank you for wanting to help, but the school answering machine would have taken a message.'

As she brushed past, Amanda caught a whiff of smoke.

'Maybe we should do this later. I've got a couple of weeks for the project.'

'That would be better, thank you dear. I need to get on and deal with this fire situation. Goodness, I hope Mrs Kingston comes back to work soon.'

Amanda slipped out as Mrs Ferris lifted the telephone receiver. She hoped that Selwyn would be true to his reputation and deny everything.

She couldn't wait to tell Gran what she'd seen in Helen's file. She also decided she needed to find out more about computers, in case it came in handy later in life. Or just in case there was ever something in her own file that might need deleting.

Amanda barely made it through the rest of the day. As soon as the final bell rang, she grabbed her bag and sprinted for the front gate.

'What's your hurry?' asked Alice.

'You'll never guess what I ...' She stopped herself, realising they were surrounded by students and parents.

Alice took her by the arm and led her to the car. When they were safely buckled into the back seat, Amanda couldn't hold it in anymore. She quickly outlined what she'd done, pausing for a word of praise from Alice, which was reluctantly given, before getting to the most interesting part.

'Helen was kicked out of her last school. And you'll never guess what for.'

'Most likely not, so best to just tell me.'

'Aren't you even going to try and guess?' Amanda's face fell.

'Did she make up stories about being attacked?'

Amanda stared at her grandmother, shocked. 'How the ... uh ...' Alice gave her a warning look, '... heck did you know that?'

'We need to work on your poker face, dear. You'd obviously found something important and based on our existing knowledge it was logical to assume it had something to do with Helen and a fake attack.'

'You take the fun out of everything,' muttered Amanda.

'We're dealing with your reputation and the police. This is not supposed to be fun, dear.'

'Well, you're right. She told her mum that a boy from school attacked her, and he got suspended and then they found out she made the whole thing up and she got expelled.'

Alice sat back and looked out the window.

'So she's done it before,' said Amanda.

'It is useful. Tell me, did the file give the name of the boy?'

Amanda blinked. 'I didn't have time to read much more. Sorry.'

'Don't be sorry Amanda. You conjured up an opportunity to

NINETEEN

gain valuable information using your wits. That is something to celebrate. Sorry is a form of regret and we don't do regret in our family.'

Amanda sighed with relief and sat up a bit straighter. Alice's was only person in the world whose opinion mattered to her. She wanted to do well because she wanted her grandmother to be proud. Alice was old and Amanda knew that a lot of her classmates' grandparents were dead already – and they had been younger than Alice. She looked at Alice and resisted the urge to lean in for a hug. Alice wasn't big on hugs.

'From which school was Helen expelled?'

'I did read that,' replied Amanda. 'She went to Northland School.'

'Interesting. She not only switched schools, she came across town. That suggests her mother wanted to give her a fresh start. What do you think our next move should be?'

Amanda had been contemplating that all afternoon. 'I think we need to find the boy she lied about.'

'Excellent.'

Amanda looked out the window. 'Where are we going? This isn't the way home.'

'We have a second mystery to solve in case you've forgotten. And so we are going to the hospital to pay our respects to Mrs Kingston.'

To Amanda that sounded like a worse plan than the time her class had done trust falls and Helen and Jenny had (predictably) failed to catch Selwyn and he'd smacked his head on the floor.

'But the police think I poisoned her. What if she thinks that as well?'

'Even more reason to visit. The sooner we set her right on that account the better.'

Amanda made several more arguments as they walked through the front entrance of Wellington Hospital.

'This is going to be really bad,' she said before clamping her mouth shut.

She rarely wanted to see her principal at school, let alone in a hospital when she possibly suspected Amanda had put her there.

'Here.' Alice handed Amanda a small box of chocolates and a bouquet of flowers.

'What are these for?'

Alice didn't bother to answer. She guided them through a narrow corridor, up some stairs, down another corridor, and finally onto a ward where Mrs Kingston was in a room by herself. Amanda expected to see her lying in bed with tubes coming out of her and machines beeping. Instead, Mrs Kingston was sitting up, wearing a brightly coloured dressing gown and reading a book. She looked pleased to see them.

'Please, come in, Alice. How are you, Amanda? This is a pleasant surprise.'

Alice nudged Amanda forward and she handed over the gifts.

'Thank you. They're beautiful. I'll get the nurse to put them into some water when she comes past.'

'How are you doing, Mrs Kingston?'

'Oh, getting there thank you, Amanda. Better than I was a few days ago that's for sure.'

Alice sat in the only visitor chair, leaving Amanda to choose between sitting on the bed, the floor, or standing. She decided to stay standing, leaning against the window frame.

'It must have been scary.'

Mrs Kingston nodded and looked like she was going to say something. Her eyes flicked to Alice.

NINETEEN

'I'll go find a vase for the flowers,' Amanda said with a smile.

She walked out of the door, turned left, then pressed herself against the wall and listened carefully.

'It was the most scared I've ever been in my life,' Mrs Kingston said. 'I thought I was having a heart attack.'

'Oh dear, you poor thing.'

Amanda smiled to herself. She'd seen Alice use the innocent old woman routine plenty of times. It never failed to get the desired response.

'Yes. My heart was racing and I felt dizzy and nauseous. I was sure I was dying.'

'And you had no warning?

'None! One moment I was sipping my drink, the next I was on my back on the floor.'

'Goodness. It's a miracle someone found you in time.'

'Thankfully Glynis came in to tell me my next appointment was ready. She called the ambulance. I'm convinced she saved my life.'

'Can I help you?'

Amanda jumped a little and turned to see a nurse standing next to her.

'I was just wanting a vase for some flowers.'

The nurse frowned suspiciously then gestured with her hand. 'Follow me.'

Reluctantly Amanda fell into step with her, wondering what she was missing.

TWENTY

Wellington, August 2021

Alice picked up her phone, then put it down again. Their agreement was that Alice would only call in an emergency. Calling to ask about something that happened twenty years ago would not count as one.

She realised she was dithering and admonished herself using language she'd learned from an American serviceman eight decades ago.

Vanessa came in and offered a distraction. 'There was nothing on the video.'

'Are you sure?'

'I'm sure. I watched it a hundred times.' She saw Alice's expression and added, 'Well, ten times. No one came through the front gate between nine last night and seven-thirty this morning when the ambulance arrived, closely followed by a police car.'

'Seven-thirty,' Alice repeated.

'Yeah, why?'

TWENTY

'Nothing, perhaps nothing. Trudy said that she discovered the body at six fifty-five. Thirty minutes seems like a long time for emergency services to respond.'

'Maybe there were other things happening in the city. Or maybe they heard there was a dead woman at a retirement village and figured it was natural causes.'

'That does seem likely,' replied Alice.

'What else did Trudy tell you?'

'That Sylvia was fully dressed, including shoes.'

'Okay so she's, she was, an early riser?'

'The shoes suggest she was about to go somewhere though.'

'Maybe for a walk.'

'Perhaps.'

'Or do you think it means something?'

'Everything means something until it doesn't.'

Vanessa rolled her eyes and poured herself a water from the jug in the fridge. 'What's our next move?'

'There's no postponing it. We need to get into her apartment.'

'And how do you propose we do that when the place is guarded by police?'

'That's not an issue.' Alice waved her hand dismissively.

'It's not?'

'No, dear. Like everything else in this world it's a matter of timing.'

'Speaking of, as I was coming up I overheard Tracey telling Kerry that Helen is due here at 2pm and to let Tracey know when she arrives.'

Alice looked at the big clock on the kitchen wall. They had three hours until Helen Gregory was due.

'She's not coming right away? Did you hear where she was coming from?'

Vanessa shook her head. 'Why?'

'No reason. Or maybe every reason. It's just another piece to the puzzle.'

'It feels like we're trying to do a puzzle without the picture.'

'Come now, it wouldn't be very challenging if you knew what you were building, would it? There's not a lot we can do about the murder until we can get into Sylvia's apartment, so I suggest we approach from a different angle. I feel like it might be time to think about moving.'

Vanessa's eyes grew wide and she opened her mouth, then closed it again and smiled. 'You almost had me. I'll make the call.'

'The number is next to the phone.'

While Vanessa called the moving company, Alice went to the window to see if there was anything of interest happening outside. A couple of residents were sunning themselves in the rose garden and she watched someone walk into the Olympic complex at the same moment as someone exited. She squinted at them as the two figures stopped and exchanged a few words.

She switched her attention to the view beyond the border of Silvermoon. Not so very long ago, the harbour had been filled with ships, bringing war weary troops home and taking fresh, innocent ones back out again. It had been a terrible time, but also the start of what had turned out to be a long and fascinating life for her.

'All set,' Vanessa said from behind her. 'Someone will be here at one.'

Alice pulled herself away from the view and nodded. 'Thank you, dear. Now, we've just enough time for a spot of planning over lunch.'

'What would you like?'

TWENTY

'I'd like you to sit down. I'll make it.'

'I don't mind,' said Vanessa.

'But I do,' Alice said firmly, as she pushed Vanessa towards the couch. 'I'm not paying you to be my nurse or cook. You learn nothing by making me lunch.'

'I don't think you've ever made me food before.'

'Then this is long overdue.'

In no time at all, Alice was plating a freshly made hash brown with bacon and fried tomatoes. Vanessa joined her and they ate at the kitchen bench.

'If I'd known you could cook like this, I would have insisted you feed me ages ago,' Vanessa said through a mouthful of food.

'Did you think I ate soup and toast for every meal?'

'No. Maybe. Part of me thought maybe you were part robot and didn't have to eat.'

'Don't be foolish.'

The grin fell from Vanessa's face as she scraped her plate clean. 'I just realised the downside to you cooking – I get to do the dishes.'

'Oh, yes. I hadn't thought of that.'

'Liar.'

'Best you hurry, our visitor will be here shortly'

Exactly at one o'clock, reception called to advise that their visitor had arrived. Alice recognised the man who was ushered into the apartment as one of the movers who'd moved Sylvia in. That told her two things. This was a small moving company, and unless he was a cold blooded murderer who'd readily returned to the scene of his crime, this man wasn't a suspect.

His thin frame reminded Alice of her own, and the dark blue eyes that roamed the room made Alice wonder if she'd found a younger version of herself.

'Harry Lyall,' he said in a low voice. His handshake was firm but not overpowering. Beneath his fifty-something frame there was a real sense of strength.

'Alice. And this is my assistant Vanessa.'

Harry nodded at them both, then sized up the room. 'You moving?'

'Thinking about it. I've made some tentative enquiries to relocate to a place up the coast. I'm just wondering about the cost.'

'How many rooms?'

'This plus the two bedrooms.'

Harry nodded. 'Can I take a look?'

Alice waved her assent and Harry went and poked his head into the spare bedroom.

'It's like he's afraid we're charging him by the word,' Vanessa whispered.

'He's measured with his words, you should pay attention,' Alice whispered back.

Harry checked the other bedroom then came back and quoted a price.

'Are you sure? That's quick to come up with a figure,' Vanessa said.

'Seen one house, seen them all,' Harry replied with a shrug.

'I'd like to talk to you about your transport insurance. I don't have too many precious items, but some of these things have sentimental value.'

'More than that.'

Alice raised her eyebrows and Harry pointed to a small statue on the bookcase. 'That's early Meissen, isn't it? Must be worth about four thousand.'

TWENTY

Then he pointed at the wooden coffee table. 'That table's eighteenth century craftsman, about three grand.'

He pointed to the picture on the wall and Alice held up her hand.

'You've made your point. Tell me, are you as careful moving them as you are at appraising their value?'

Harry shrugged. 'Too many people try and overvalue their stuff so they can make me pay if it gets broken.'

'What about Sylvia Kingston? Did she try and overvalue her... stuff?'

Harry blinked a couple of times and sucked on his teeth. 'Only dealt with her granddaughter. She didn't ask me about insurance.'

'Is that usual?' asked Vanessa.

Harry rubbed the side of his face while he considered his reply. 'Yep.'

'Do you have someone that works with you? I saw another man with you when you came the other day.'

For the first time emotion crossed Harry's face. 'That bugger didn't show up for work. Left me high and dry.'

'Oh dear. How frustrating for you.'

Harry clamped his mouth shut.

'Did you know Sylvia was attacked the morning after she moved in?'

Harry's mouth stayed closed but his eyes flicked to Alice and he gave a small nod.

'Because the police came and asked you about it?'

Another nod.

'Please understand, as you've said, I do have some valuable things, and it looks to me like your employee saw the things Sylvia had and came back to take one or two for himself.'

There was silence for a long time, then Harry sighed. 'I only had him as a favour. He's my cousin's brother-in-law. Lazy, entitled. Thinks the world owes him.'

'Sounds like you are well rid of him,' Alice replied. 'I only hope what he's done doesn't impact your business.'

Harry's scowl suggested he'd already thought of that.

'What's his name? I think it's important for people like me to know who to stay away from.' Alice smiled sweetly. It made her face hurt with the artificialness of it all.

Harry mulled over the question for a while before replying. 'Marty Stanley. He's not as strong or as smart as he thinks he is.'

'Most people aren't.'

Harry grinned at Alice, then looked thoughtful. 'I'll tell you what I told the cops. He's a sneaky sod. Might pinch something, but he'd never thump a woman.'

'Chivalry?'

'Nah, fear. His mum is dead set scary. If she found out he'd hit a woman she'd drive him to the cop station herself.'

'Sounds like my sort of woman.'

Harry grinned again. 'You and her'd probably get on alright.'

'Will the police find him?'

'Probably. They're smarter than him.'

Harry stood up and nodded to them both before starting for the door.

'Don't you want to discuss the move?'

He paused and looked over his shoulder. 'Nah, you ain't moving.'

'How can you tell?' asked Vanessa.

'Doing this for thirty years. Get to know the vibe of someone moving. You don't have it.'

TWENTY

Alice stood up and met him at the front door.

'Don't you want to know why I asked you to come if I wasn't planning on moving?'

Harry shook his head. 'Not my business.'

Alice held out her hand and he took it. 'Harry Lyall, it was a pleasure to meet you.'

He nodded to Vanessa and left.

'Weirdo,' Vanessa said.

'Not at all. I wish more people were less curious. And now we've got a name.'

'Marty Stanley. But we don't know where he is or how to find him.'

'Which is…'

'A problem.'

'No Vanessa. If you learn nothing else from me then remember this. Lack of information isn't a problem, it's a challenge. We simply don't know something that we need to know, so how do we find it out?'

'Do you think Marty killed Sylvia?'

'No. In fact right now I'm not convinced he even attacked her.'

'Then why are we going to this trouble … sorry, uh … effort to find him?'

'Because I'm not one hundred percent sure. He's the logical choice, especially in light of what Harry just told us of the man's character. And someone did come onto the property that night. So in the absence of any other clues, we'll start with finding Marty Stanley.'

'How?'

Alice didn't reply but her smile made Vanessa shift uncomfortably on her chair.

TWENTY-ONE

Wellington, March 1994

'This makes me nervous.'

'More nervous than visiting your principal in hospital?'

Amanda shuffled her feet and looked up at the white wooden house. 'That was way different. Anyway, you did most of the talking there.'

'Helen appears to want to patch things up between the two of you. Why else would she have sent you a note?'

Amanda's fingers twitched towards her pocket, but she didn't pull out the folded piece of paper. She had memorised the message anyway.

Amanda. Sorry for all the stuff that's happened. Could we start over? Come to my house at eleven on Saturday morning. Helen

Amanda had found the note in her school bag, which was also weird because Helen was still off school. Her first instinct had been to throw the note away, but then Alice had found it and insisted they go.

'But why?' she'd said.

TWENTY-ONE

'You know why,' Alice had replied.

She had known why but she didn't like it.

Even worse, Alice had insisted Amanda dress up. She hated wearing dresses, they were so uncomfortable. When she'd questioned Alice about it, she'd begrudgingly accepted the explanation that being seen to make an effort was often more important than making an actual effort. And put the other person at ease and more likely to make a mistake. Amanda didn't really understand the first bit but definitely did the second.

'Off you go,' Alice said.

Amanda grimaced and started up the path. After a few steps she realised Alice wasn't with her. 'Aren't you coming?'

'The note was addressed to you,' Alice replied.

'But …' Amanda took a step back towards the gate.

'Go, learn something.'

'Learn what?'

'I don't know. At the very least try and resolve this silly feud between the two of you. I'd rather not have the police on my front doorstep again.'

Amanda thought it was a bad idea, but she knew it was a waste of time arguing with Alice, so she stomped up the path to the front door and rang the bell.

She waited.

When no one came to the door, she rang the bell again and glanced over her shoulder at Alice. Getting no encouragement, she knocked on the door as loudly as she could.

There was a click and the door swung open.

Beyond the open door she saw a hallway stretching towards the back of the house. A few doors lined both sides of the hall, some open and others closed.

'Hello? Helen?'

Amanda took a hesitant step through the door and called again. She listened but there was no sound from inside the house. She stepped back onto the porch and pulled the door firmly closed.

'No one's home,' she said, returning to Alice at the gate.

'Curious,' replied Alice.

'Curious? What does that mean?'

'What do you think it means?'

Amanda groaned. 'Can't you just answer a question straight for once?'

'I did. I asked you what you think it means?'

'I don't know,' Amanda said through gritted teeth. 'That's why I'm asking you.'

Alice waited. The expression on her face made Amanda feel small and frustrated and furious. It was like Alice was challenging her to use her brain, while calling her stupid at the same time.

'She's playing a trick on me. She wanted me to show up and make an idiot of myself.'

'And that would mean …?'

'That would mean,' Amanda continued slowly, 'that she's watching me right now. Otherwise, what's the point?' She looked around, half expecting Helen to jump out from behind a bush. 'She's messing with me.'

Before they could say anything else, a police car turned into the street and screeched to a stop in the driveway beside them. Two officers jumped out.

'Hold it right there!'

'Is there a problem, Officer?' asked Alice.

One officer pushed past Amanda and strode up the path. He

TWENTY-ONE

hammered on the front door, then opened it.

'Have either of you been inside this house?' asked the second officer.

'No,' Alice replied. 'What's the matter?'

'We got a call about a break-in.'

'Well, we are both clearly standing outside the property.'

The first officer reappeared at the front door and beckoned for them to join him. 'There's no one inside, but the place has been tossed.'

Amanda rolled her eyes. *Not again. I have the worst luck.*

'Are you sure neither of you have been in the house?'

'Officer, do I strike you as the sort of person who would break into a house, then stand at the front gate and chat about it?'

'Then you won't mind me searching you?'

'I wouldn't recommend it.'

'Is that a threat?' The officer took a step towards Alice, dwarfing her in height and weight.

Amanda looked from her grandmother to the police officer and back again. Sparring in a dojo was one thing, but she'd never fought in real life. Amanda wasn't sure she could take this officer, but if he laid a hand on Alice, she'd definitely give it a try. Carefully she slid one foot back and bent her knees a fraction.

'A threat?' Alice laughed. 'How am I in a position to threaten you? I mean look at me and look at you. I'm just saying I know my rights. You found my granddaughter and I outside the property. I've told you that we never entered the house. You have no reason to search us.'

The officer scratched at the stubble on his chin as he looked her up and down. 'You might be right. Except the triple one

Antiques and Assault

call said a young girl had broken into the house.'

He looked at Amanda. 'Maybe your grandmother didn't go inside, but I'll bet you did. Perhaps she was the lookout while you nipped inside. Is that what happened?' His voice was filled with condescension.

Amanda stood tall and shook her head. 'No,' she replied clearly. 'This is the house of someone I know from school.'

She'd said the wrong thing.

'So you've been here before! Maybe you scoped some things out and decided to come back and help yourself when you knew she wouldn't be around.'

Amanda stared at him. 'I'm twelve. I don't scope things out. Besides, I was invited.' She thrust the note into his hand and tapped her foot impatiently while he read it.

'Doesn't mean anything,' the officer said. 'You could have written this yourself.'

Alice plucked the note from his hand and slipped it into her pocket. 'While this is a fascinating conversation, I'm feeling a little tired. I think we'd better be going now.'

She turned and the officer put his hand out. 'Not until I say you can go.'

Amanda waited for her to do something, to say something, to blow up at him or to flip him off the step using her karate skills. Instead Alice gave him a look that Amanda had never seen before. She couldn't even properly describe it, but she was glad Alice had never had cause to give her that look.

Several seconds passed in silence before the officer removed his hand and mumbled.

His partner smiled gently at Alice. 'If we could have your names and your address so we can get in touch with you if we need to.'

TWENTY-ONE

Alice gave the officer their information then took Amanda's hand and walked her away from the house. 'Don't look back,' she murmured.

As they greeted their driver and climbed into the back of the car, Alice said conversationally, 'Now, wasn't that interesting.'

'No! Why do you always think scary things are interesting?'

'Were you scared?'

Amanda took a deep breath and let it out slowly. 'Okay, not scared, but it wasn't a good thing that just happened.'

'Wasn't it? We know more than we did before.'

Amanda took another breath and ran through the list again. 'Helen set me up. She sent me the note, knowing she wasn't going to be home, then she called the cops and said I was breaking in.'

'Which means?'

'Which means,' Amanda repeated slowly, 'which means she was definitely watching me arrive.'

Alice nodded. 'That would seem likely. Although?'

Amanda's mind raced as she thought through all the possibilities. 'She didn't actually need to be there. The note said to come at eleven. She just needed to wait until eleven and call the police. What if I hadn't shown up though?'

'I suspect it didn't matter whether you were there or not. The call got the attention of the police. I believe we'll get another visit from them shortly to say that the owners of the house came home and confirmed there were several items missing.'

'But we didn't do anything.'

'We were there and that's enough to throw suspicion in our direction. But they have no proof so there's nothing to worry about, dear.'

Despite these assurances, Amanda did worry all the way

home. Some lunch and homework helped distract her from the morning's events, but when there was a loud knock on the front door all her anxiety rushed back.

It was horrible Detective Graves and quiet Constable Wilson. The detective got straight into it.

'At five minutes past eleven this morning a patrol car responded to a 111 report of a burglary in process. Upon their arrival the two of you were located outside the property, whereupon Amanda informed the officers that the house belonged to Helen Gregory, a classmate, and victim of a recent assault.'

'Yes,' Alice replied. 'We know.'

Detective Graves scowled at her interruption. 'Subsequent to that, we received an anonymous tip that Amanda had broken into the Gregory house and stole a small gold bracelet.'

'An anonymous tip? Really?' asked Alice.

'You were there.'

'But I didn't go into the house,' protested Amanda.

'So you say. Are there any witnesses that can verify that? Apart from your grandmother?'

Amanda shook her head.

'Would you mind if we take a look around, just to make sure?'

'Yes I would mind. Do you have a search warrant?' Alice asked.

Graves locked eyes with Alice, but he was the first to look away.

'Of course we can get one. I was just hoping we could resolve this without needing to go all official. After all, if Amanda stole it and returns it, there may not be any need to take it further.'

His voice was friendly but Amanda was watching his eyes. They didn't look friendly.

TWENTY-ONE

'For example, there are many places to hide a stolen bracelet, such as beneath her bed or inside her shoe,' Graves continued, his eyes now boring into Amanda.

'Amanda, dear, show the man your shoes.'

Her heart thumping, Amanda took her shoes off and tipped them upside down to show there was nothing inside.

'Not those shoes, obviously,' Graves said.

'We're just trying to eliminate Amanda as a suspect,' Wilson said.

Unlike the older detective, Amanda found she liked the young constable. He had a face she thought she could trust.

'An innocent person would bend over backwards to prove their innocence.'

'This isn't about her innocence or guilt though, is it?' Alice said with a grim smile. 'This is about two grown men wanting to poke around in a young girl's bedroom.'

'Now hang on—'

'I have been raising my granddaughter by myself since she was a baby and I take her safety seriously. So come back with a warrant, or don't come back at all. Someone obviously has a grudge against Amanda so I suggest you turn your attention to discovering whoever that might be. Or perhaps I ought to telephone the newspapers and let them know that my twelve-year-old granddaughter is being harassed by the police.'

Graves' face turned red and Amanda worried that he was going to have a heart attack. Instead he stood up and took a step towards Alice.

'This isn't over,' he said through clenched teeth.

Alice slowly got to her feet. She was still considerably shorter than the detective. Meanwhile Constable Wilson stood and placed a hand on his colleague's shoulder.

'I'll have a warrant within the hour. Don't leave home.'

Alice and Amanda accompanied them to the front door.

As soon as the door was closed and locked, Alice spun to face Amanda. 'Check your shoes.'

'I did.'

'Not those ones, the ones in your wardrobe. Now! Check them all.'

Amanda raced into her room and checked inside every shoe. She didn't find anything.

'Is that all of them?' Alice asked from the doorway.

'Yes.'

'Are you sure?'

Amanda looked into her wardrobe again. She didn't have many pairs of shoes. Her eyes widened. 'My netball shoes.'

'Where are they?'

'Back porch.'

Alice walked quickly through the house to the back door, closely followed by Amanda. Amanda's shoes were resting on the top step. The right shoe was silent when Alice shook it. When she shook the left shoe, it rattled. Alice put her hand into it and pulled out a gold bracelet.

'I swear, I've never seen that before.'

Alice examined the bracelet thoughtfully. 'I know you haven't, dear.'

TWENTY-TWO

Wellington, August 2021

'This isn't clever, dear, this is straight forward.'

'It's only straight forward if we don't get caught.'

Alice didn't reply. She knew everything was straight forward as long as you didn't get caught.

At precisely two o'clock she and Vanessa approached the apartment next to Sylvia Gregory's. She briefly smiled at the police officer guarding Sylvia's door and he nodded in return.

Suddenly there was a loud screeching and the sound of smashing glass and metal. Everyone turned towards the sound which came from the front of the main building.

The officer took a step forward then looked back at the door he was guarding.

'Oh dear. I hope no one was badly hurt,' Alice said loudly.

The officer took off in a run. Alice waited and watched until he turned the corner, then, using the key Vanessa had obtained from Tracey's office, they unlocked Sylvia's door and slipped inside.

Antiques and Assault

'How long do you think we have?' asked Vanessa.

'As long as we need. Getting in was easy, getting out again will be a bit trickier.'

Vanessa sighed and muttered something under her breath.

'Less complaining, more searching.'

'What am I even searching for?'

'I'm not certain,' Alice admitted as she scanned the room. 'Something that's here that shouldn't be, or something that isn't here that should be.'

'Thank you, Alice. That's a big help,' Vanessa replied.

Alice stepped into the middle of the room and conjured a picture in her mind of the first time she'd been in the room. She wasn't sure exactly what she was looking for, except perhaps a motive.

'If something is missing then it points to theft as the motive for Sylvia's murder. If everything is still here then there's something else behind Sylvia's death. You look in here, I'll check the bedroom.'

She walked into the bedroom. Everything was neat and tidy. Alice pushed open the wardrobe door and found the clothes rack empty. Several boxes were stacked on the floor. She pulled the flaps of the top box open and saw scrunched up newspaper. Beneath the newspaper, she found an object wrapped in tissue paper. Carefully she lifted the object out and placed it on the bed before unwrapping it.

The small figurine of an angel was breathtakingly beautiful. And strangely familiar. She checked the bottom and found a small B scratched into the base, confirming her suspicions. She fumbled for her phone and took a photo, then she rewrapped it and returned it to the box. She unwrapped two more items from inside the box. Both packages contained small

TWENTY-TWO

porcelain bowls. Those she didn't recognise, but she took photos anyway.

'I found something,' Vanessa said from the doorway.

Alice quickly returned the wrapped bowls to the box and slid the wardrobe door closed. Vanessa was holding a grey bag.

'There's a laptop bag, but I can't find the computer anywhere.'

'Perhaps it's an old bag and she got rid of the laptop.'

Vanessa shook her head and held the bag open for Alice to look inside.

'The cords are still here. And it was next to the couch. If it was old it would have been hidden in some cupboard.'

'Good observation. Now put it back before someone notices you've moved it.'

While Vanessa did that, Alice went to the bedside tables. The one on the left had nothing on it or in the drawers. An alarm clock and a glass of water sat on the right side table. In the drawer she found a bible and a small container of pills. Alice took a photo of the pill bottle, then flicked through the bible. She'd once opened a bible and found a concealed Derringer pistol, but alas this one held no such secrets. She closed the drawer. Then she had a thought and checked the alarm clock. It was set for 7.30am but wasn't switched on.

'Alice, the cop is coming back,' Vanessa called from the other room.

Alice looked through the bedroom window and saw the officer walking back towards the apartment. She sent a text, and a few seconds later there was a loud bang overhead, drawing the officer's attention. When he looked back down, Alice and Vanessa were walking in his direction.

'It's a bit early in the day for fireworks,' Alice said.

'Sure is. Bit early in the year too,' the officer replied with a smile.

As they passed the parking lot, Alice gave Joshua a thumbs up. The parttime groundskeeper and Alice's occasional assistant had been happy to devise a distraction with a movie sound effect, a portable speaker and a leftover firework.

Joshua grinned and waved, then ducked behind a car.

'How did you know that would work?'

'Most things will if they're timed just right.'

'Fair enough. So, apart from a missing laptop, did we learn anything?'

'It's a nice day, dear. Why don't we sit out in the rose garden for a bit.'

Vanessa looked at her suspiciously. 'You hate sitting and you hate smelly flowers.'

'I hate staring at the same four walls more. A change of scenery might help get the brain cells working.'

They sat on a bench seat with the sun on their faces. It was warm without being hot and all the roses were just beginning to bloom, so the scent wasn't overpowering. Alice couldn't bear the garden in the middle of summer, but at this time of the year she was surprised to find it was quite pleasant.

'Sylvia was found fully dressed before seven o'clock. The alarm in her bedroom was set for half seven, and it was switched off.'

'Maybe she woke early and decided to get up anyway.'

'It's possible. It's also possible that she was woken by somebody.'

'I didn't see anyone on the security camera footage. You don't think it was someone living at Silvermoon, do you?'

Alice watched a sparrow land on the top of the fence. Its

TWENTY-TWO

head swivelled from side to side looking for danger. Alice sympathised with it.

'I'd like to say no, but let's face it, the last couple of years would increase the odds of it being otherwise. Still, my instincts tell me that this has nothing to do with Silvermoon. Sylvia Gregory was targeted. I just don't know yet by whom or why. I wish…'

'What?'

'Let's imagine Sylvia wasn't expecting to get up when she did. What prompted her to get dressed?'

Vanessa jumped up from her seat and began to pace. She did her best thinking when she was moving (a habit that Alice was trying to train her out of).

'Someone came to the door… or someone called her?'

Alice nodded. 'If we had her phone we could know for sure.'

'I assume the police have it. Do you think Troy might be able to work his magic and access her phone records?'

Troy knew more about electronics than probably the rest of the city combined, and he wasn't averse to employing less than legal methods to assist Alice on occasion. But Vanessa got all giggly and flirty around him, and even though Alice liked Troy, she knew he wasn't the relationship type and she was determined to keep her protégé at a distance from him.

'Perhaps, but there's something else.' She told Vanessa about the box in Sylvia's wardrobe.

'So she hadn't unpacked some stuff,' Vanessa responded with a shrug.

'The B on the bottom stands for Bartholdi. He was a French sculptor from the late 18th century. His work is worth tens of thousands.'

Vanessa whistled, then looked embarrassed. 'Okay, but that

Antiques and Assault

doesn't mean much. She has some expensive stuff. But so do you if that moving guy was right.'

'That's not my point. There aren't many Bartholdi pieces left in the world. They're rare enough that I would be surprised if someone like Sylvia could afford one.'

Vanessa kept pacing. 'There could be any number of logical explanations. She might be richer than we think. Or it might be a family heirloom.'

'Both strong possibilities.'

'But?'

'But someone with that much wealth doesn't employee a two-man moving company. They go top of the line.'

'She could have been rich and tight with money.'

Alice sighed. Too many possibilities. 'How do you feel about doing some more research?'

Vanessa's expression told her exactly what she thought of it.

'If I could do it I would, but you know I can't use the computer thing like you can.'

'Every time you use the word *thing* to describe something I thinking I'm being conned.'

'I don't know what you're talking about, dear.'

'Mmm-hmm.'

As they started back towards Alice's apartment a car crawled through the main gate and stopped outside the main door. Helen Gregory climbed from the driver's seat and walked up the stairs, carrying a small suitcase.

Alice quickened her pace and pushed through the doors where she found Helen standing at the reception desk. A small notice indicated that the concierge was temporarily away.

'Helen,' Alice called out.

She turned and an irritated look flashed across her face

TWENTY-TWO

before being replaced with one of sadness. 'Yes?'

'Alice. We met when your grandmother moved in.' Alice walked over and pressed Helen's hand between her own. 'I'm so sorry for your loss.'

'Thank you, it's been a terrible shock. I was told to see the manager when I got here rather than going straight to my grandmother's apartment.'

'Why don't I take you over to the apartment and Vanessa can wait for Tracey. I'm sure she won't be long.'

Helen hesitated then gave a slight nod. 'Thank you.'

'Would you like to leave your suitcase here? Vanessa can watch it for you. I'm sure you don't want to have to carry it around.'

'Are you sure?'

'Of course. We don't know how much walking you'll need to do to get dear Sylvia's affairs in order and it could get quite heavy.'

'I guess. If you're sure it's alright.'

Vanessa smiled warmly. 'Absolutely fine. I'll pop it behind the desk and wait right here until Tracey comes back.'

Helen dithered a little more, then placed the black hard-shelled suitcase behind the desk. Alice noticed it was closed by two locks.

'I only met Sylvia briefly, but she seemed like a lovely woman,' Alice said, guiding Helen out of the door.

'Thank you, she was a good grandmother. I don't know what I'll do without her.'

'What about the rest of your family? Are they local?'

Helen shook her head. 'It's just me and Sylvia ... *was* just me and Sylvia.'

'I'm so sorry.'

'Thank you.'

They walked in silence to where the police officer was still on duty.

'I'm Helen Gregory. This is my grandmother's residence. I would like to see inside.'

'I'm sorry, Ms Gregory. I can't let anyone in.'

'You can't let anyone in ...' Helen repeated, leaning forward as if waiting for the constable to complete the sentence.

'... to the apartment?'

'... without permission,' said Helen. 'You can't let anyone in without permission.'

'No ma'am.'

'Well?'

The constable looked at Alice helplessly and she was about to intervene when Helen spoke again.

'Well, then get permission. Call whoever you need to.'

The constable pulled out his phone and quickly made a call. While he spoke in a low voice, Helen kept her eyes firmly on him. Every time he looked at her, he saw her stern expression. It was a good trick, and one that Alice had used plenty of times.

She watched Helen out of the corner of her eye. Despite the stern telling off she'd just given the officer, her hands were twitching and she was shifting her weight.

The rational side of Alice said that it was natural for Helen to be nervous about going into her dead grandmother's apartment, especially when she had been murdered. The suspicious side of Alice wondered if there was more to it.

'The lead detective will be here in thirty minutes. He would like you to wait.'

Helen's shoulders started to shake and Alice thought she was about punch the police officer. Then Helen started to cry.

TWENTY-TWO

'I'm sorry. This is stressful and I've travelled a long way to get here and I just want to be in her home again. To be surrounded by her things so that I could maybe, just for a moment, feel like she's still with me.'

The constable put the phone to his ear and murmured something.

'You can go in, but I have to accompany you.'

'Of course,' Helen sniffed.

The constable slipped his phone in a pocket and unlocked the front door.

Helen turned to Alice. 'Thank you, Alice. I won't keep you anymore.'

Alice smiled. 'It's no problem. Are you sure you're going to be alright? You don't want me to stay for moral support.'

'Er, no I'll be fine, thank you. I'll be along to fetch my suitcase from reception shortly.'

Alice waited until she'd disappeared through the door with the constable before retreating. Helen had given her food for thought. Grieving granddaughter or cunning manipulator? The jury was still out.

Vanessa was sitting behind the reception desk, phone to her ear. She hung up as Alice walked in.

'Thank you for saving me from this life,' Vanessa said.

'Not enjoying the trip down memory lane?'

'Honestly I don't know how I stayed on reception for as long as I did. And I'd love to know where Kerry is. I don't remember ever leaving my desk for as long as she has.'

'I'm sure she isn't far away. Any sign of Tracey?'

Vanessa shook her head. 'Maybe they're in a meeting together.'

'Possibly. Why don't you knock on Tracey's office door while

I keep an eye on reception.'

'You're going to watch reception?'

'Why not? It doesn't appear difficult.'

'Uh huh.' Vanessa stood up and gestured for Alice to take her seat.

'Right lock is done,' she said, before exiting through the door to the hallway containing the offices.

Alice grinned when she saw Helen's suitcase lying flat on the floor. As Vanessa said, the right side lock was open. It took Alice ten seconds with a paper clip to open the left side lock. Quickly she flipped open the lid.

'Well, well, well …'

TWENTY-THREE

Wellington, March 1994

Detective Graves stood on the doorstep with a piece of paper giving him the authority to enter and search the house. Constable Wilson stood quietly behind him looking faintly embarrassed.

'Move aside please, Mrs Strong,' Graves said triumphantly.

Amanda waited for Alice to tell him to go away. Instead she plucked the search warrant from his hands and scanned it. With a faint smile, she handed it back and stepped aside to let the policemen into the house.

They went straight down the hallway into Amanda's bedroom. Amanda followed and watched from the doorway as Graves opened her wardrobe door and searched inside each of her shoes. After a minute he stood and scanned the room.

'Search under the bed,' he said.

Wilson got on his hands and knees and looked up the bed, then shook his head.

'Are there any other shoes in the house belonging to you?'

Amanda began to shake her head then stopped. 'My netball shoes are on the back door step.'

Graves pushed past and she resisted the urge to kick him in the bum. He returned shortly, disappointment and frustration creasing his face.

'Alright, I was hoping you'd make it easy, but we'll do this the hard way. Constable, tear this place apart.'

'Sir.'

'I don't think so,' Alice said calmly.

Graves pulled out the warrant and waved it at her. 'This says we can do what we like.'

'Actually,' replied Alice, 'it's a bit more specific than that.'

Graves stared at her, then opened the warrant and read it. His cheeks darkened and he gripped the paper so tightly his fingers tore the edges.

'I do wonder something,' Alice said. 'Why is a detective involved in a suspected theft?'

Graves glared at her. 'I don't have to answer to you. Come on.'

He marched down the hall and out the front door without another word.

'Why did they leave?' asked Amanda.

'In his haste to get the warrant, Detective Graves was too specific. He was authorised to come in and search your shoes. There was no mention about the rest of the house.'

A knock at the door interrupted further conversation.

When Alice opened it, Constable Wilson stood on the doorstep, hat in hands.

'Ma'am. Officially I'm here to advise you to stay close for when we come back. Unofficially I'd like to apologise for my colleague. Detective Graves is under a great deal of pressure

TWENTY-THREE

to solve this case. Assaults on minors are high profile.'

'You still think that Amanda assaulted Helen Gregory?'

Wilson played with his hat as he replied. 'We were pursuing other areas of enquiry until we got the tip about Helen's bracelet.'

'How?'

Wilson blinked. 'Excuse me?'

'How did you get the tip?'

Wilson blinked again and Amanda could almost see him mouthing the question.

'Detective Graves came ready to bust down my door and tear my house apart looking for something based on an anonymous tip?'

Wilson pursed his lips then nodded.

'Don't you find it a little odd that Graves is reacting so strongly to something that could be completely fabricated?'

'We move quickly on any information.'

'I'll ask again, how did you receive the tip?'

'I'm sorry, ma'am. I can't reveal that.'

'I understand. Still, phone calls can be easy to misinterpret.'

'It wasn't a... I can assure you the message was clear. Are you aware of anyone who might have a grudge against Amanda?'

'There are a few children that don't like her, but none that would take things this far.'

'Okay, well, I'm sorry for the inconvenience.' Wilson started to turn away, then looked back. 'Detective Graves has a reputation. Once he gets his teeth into something, he rarely lets go.'

'I'll take that under advisement,' Alice replied. 'Thank you, Constable.'

As he walked down the path, Alice muttered, 'I'm going to

have to watch that Graves. He's going to be trouble.' Then, with a shake of her head and a wry smile, she winked at Amanda. 'Lucky I'm retired.'

'What the heck?' Amanda said from the living room doorway. 'Why is everyone out to get me?'

'Think, Amanda. Better yet, eat something, then think. Thinking on an empty stomach is like trying to solve a problem with half your brain tied behind your back.'

'Is that even a saying?'

'It is now.'

Alice marched into the kitchen and made a sandwich with the last two slices of bread and some strawberry jam, they were the only things in the fridge less than a month old.

'Okay, first things first. We need to go to the supermarket.'

'Agreed.'

'Secondly, tomorrow you're going to school to find out who put the supposed note from Helen into your bag.'

'How am I going to do that?'

'By ruling out who it couldn't have been.'

Amanda opened her mouth to ask another question, then closed it again. She took a bite instead and then said through a mouthful of sandwich, 'by eliminating all the people that didn't have access to my bag, I'm identifying the only people it could be.'

'Which should be a much smaller pool of people.'

'But how do I know who did it?'

'That's when you move onto the second part of the equation. Motive. Why would they want to put the note in your bag?'

Amanda finished the rest of the sandwich, wiping her face with the back of her hand, which elicited a sigh from Alice.

'Sorry,' Amanda mumbled. She plucked a tissue out of the

TWENTY-THREE

box on the counter and delicately wiped her face clean. 'But the person who did it isn't just going to tell me because I asked.'

'That's true. But you have a big advantage in your quest for answers.'

'I do? What's that?'

Alice grinned. 'You're in a school. The only thing that spreads faster through school than rumours is head lice.'

'Gross.'

'My point is, you don't need to ask everybody, just ask the right question to the right person and let them do the rest.'

'How will I know who that is?'

'I think you probably already know.'

'Would it kill you to just tell me?'

TWENTY-FOUR

Wellington, August 2021

'Would it kill you to just tell me?' Vanessa said.

They were back in Alice's apartment, having located Tracey and pointed her in the direction of Helen Gregory.

'I want you to use your brain.'

Vanessa threw her hands up in disgust. 'Fine! The case contained a magical portal to a land of monsters.'

'What? Don't be ridiculous.'

'It held a disassembled sniper rifle. Helen is an international assassin.'

Alice snorted. 'You do know the difference between your brain and your imagination, don't you?'

'How am I supposed to know? You came back before I could get it open.'

'Yes, well we'll work on that later. You should have had it open before Helen and I reached the bottom step.'

Vanessa scowled and muttered something under her breath.

'Think. How did she carry the suitcase? How did it feel

TWENTY-FOUR

when you put it behind the desk? What was missing?'

'Whoa, hang on, one thing at a time.' Vanessa began pacing the room, until Alice snapped at her to sit down.

'But I think better when I'm moving.'

'You're not a hamster on a wheel. Think stationary.'

Reluctantly Vanessa sat on the couch and took a deep breath. 'Okay, how was she carrying it? By the handle.'

'How was she walking?'

Vanessa looked at Alice like she'd gone mad. 'With her feet.'

Alice bit back sarcasm and waited.

'Alright, how did she walk?' Vanessa said to herself. 'She put one foot in front of the …'

'Yes?' prompted Alice.

'She was walking normally.'

'And?'

'Oh, I get it. She shouldn't have been. When I'm carrying a full suitcase, I'm all over the place, it bangs into my legs and throws me off course.'

Alice smiled. 'What else?'

'When she handed it to me it felt heavy, like a suitcase should, but now that I think about it, it wasn't as heavy as a case filled with clothes would be.' She looked at Alice excitedly.

'And what was missing?'

'Missing,' Vanessa repeated. Her legs jiggled up and down and Alice could tell she was dying to pace. 'I don't know.'

Alice relaxed into her seat. It was often harder to recall what wasn't there.

'I don't know about you, but when I get home from a flight I unpack the suitcase and put it in the wardrobe. What I don't do is take off the—'

'Baggage tags!'

'Yes.'

'And there were no baggage tags on Helen's suitcase. No name tag either.'

'Right. Now it's possible that she ripped them off when she got off the flight. But are we supposed to believe that Helen was so grief stricken about Sylvia's death that she jumped on the first available plane, and rushed straight here from the airport? If you're in that much of a hurry, would you take the time to remove airline tags from your suitcase?'

'Nope. So she was lying about coming from the airport. So why bring the suitcase at all?'

'Why would you bring a case somewhere? To bring something along.'

Vanessa couldn't contain herself any longer. She jumped up and walked to the window and back again. 'Or to take something away?'

Alice nodded. 'Helen's suitcase was filled with that bubbled plasticy stuff. You know, the stuff they wrap around fragile things.'

'Bubble wrap.'

'Yes, what's it called?'

'Bubble wrap.'

'Oh. The inventors didn't waste a lot of thought on that name did they.'

'Well, the only reason to bring bubble wrap is if you're intending to take something away. Something you don't want to get damaged.'

Alice sighed and closed her eyes. She was tired and her ankle ached.

'Alice?'

'What?' Alice replied in a warning tone.

TWENTY-FOUR

'Would you like something to eat?'

'Oh,' Alice opened her eyes, 'yes, actually, that would be nice.'

While Vanessa prepared a sandwich, Alice thought.

'I believe this has all been the work of one person. The assault, the murder. And now Helen itching to take something from Sylvia's apartment. '

'So Helen beat up her own grandmother, then killed her? Why?'

'Good question. The killing I can understand.'

'Oh really?'

'You know what I mean,' Alice said impatiently. 'They fought, Helen lashed out. Crime of passion. It's plausible. But assaulting her first, then killing her a few days later. It doesn't make sense.'

'It doesn't?'

'If Helen killed Sylvia and was so worried about removing something from the apartment that she brought a suitcase back to a crime scene, why didn't she just take the item when the murder occurred?'

Vanessa paused pacing to take a bite of sandwich, then continued her loop. 'Does that mean Helen didn't kill her grandmother?'

Alice sighed. 'I don't know, yet. But remember Sylvia's visit here? She was worried, almost scared. Sylvia said *she* would be angry with her, and there was something she didn't want to do anymore. I have a feeling that's the key to this whole thing.'

They finished the rest of their sandwiches in silence then, despite Vanessa's protest, Alice cleared the plates and put them into the dishwasher. Sometimes movement helped her think.

'How about a little reconnaissance?' Alice said.

'As long as that's not a fancy word for research, I'm all for it.'

'I need you to spy on Tracey and Helen.'

Vanessa was off her seat so fast the stool wobbled perilously close to falling over. 'Be back later.'

She was out the door before Alice could give further instructions.

Alice shook her head. She knew research was boring, but it was essential. Perhaps she was too rigid with her training. A little more variety could be the ticket to keeping the young girl interested.

There was a rattling sound and Alice watched her phone buzz on the coffee table. She checked the display and answered it with a smile.

'I thought you were working.'

'I am,' Amanda replied. 'But I've got time for a check in with my favourite grandmother.'

'I'm your only grandmother.'

'How are you?'

'I'm fine. Which is more than can be said for our newest resident.'

'Oh no, don't tell me you picked a fight with Helen Gregory's grandmother.'

'No, but someone did.' She filled Amanda in on the events of the last few days.

'Wow, no one is going to want to live at Silvermoon soon.'

'Don't say *wow*. I raised you better than that.'

Amanda's laugh echoed down the phone line and Alice felt her lips twitch.

'Do you need me?' asked Amanda.

'No. I've got Vanessa in case things turn pear-shaped.'

'Gee thanks, Gran. Way to make a girl feel wanted.'

'Don't call me gran.'

TWENTY-FOUR

'Alright, you old grump. Do you need anything from me?'

'What do you remember about Helen?'

'Except from the fact that she was an evil, manipulative little sod? Why? You think she's involved?'

'Right up to her diamond earrings. I just can't quite figure out exactly how.'

'You'll work it out.'

In the background Alice heard an announcement and a soft bell ding. 'Where are you?'

'I'm at the theatre. Got to go. It'll be a couple of days before I can check in again. Don't die in the meantime.'

'Same to you.'

It was their alternative to saying 'I love you'. Alice knew if she ever told Amanda she loved her, Amanda would be on the first flight home, convinced her grandmother was taking her last breaths.

She wished she could remember more about the incident with Helen Gregory at Amanda's primary school. She had a feeling it might hold a clue as to what was happening now. But her memories were hazy at best and she'd only met the girl once or twice. Amanda had sorted it out at the time. Alice recalled mainly offering advice and guidance.

A knock at the door pulled her back from memory lane. She checked the security camera via her phone and saw Owen standing in the hallway.

'This is a nice surprise,' she said when she opened the door. 'We hadn't scheduled anything had we?'

'No,' Owen replied with a smile of his own. 'I thought I'd come by and take Vanessa up on her offer to assist with this speech I'm giving.'

'Oh, she's just popped out, but shouldn't be long. Would you like a cup of tea while you wait?'

'No, thank you, I just had one.'

They settled into the living room and Alice asked, 'Owen, you never got around to telling me what your speech is about.'

'Ah yes, we were interrupted. It seems some fool has got it into their head that a lifetime of working for a bank qualifies me to give retirees advise on how to avoid scams.'

'Why on Earth did you agree to do it?'

Owen hesitated, his cheeks turning a light shade of pink. 'Well, … it was very nice to be asked.'

'I understand.'

'You do?' Owen replied in a relieved tone.

'Of course. You were flattered by the invitation. You jumped first, and thought after.'

'Roughly, yes. And now I have to do a streaming thing. I'm not even sure what a streaming thing is, but supposedly there could be hundreds of people watching.'

'I wouldn't worry, if they all have the same level of internet knowledge as you, most of them probably won't be able to work out how to watch.'

'Thank you, Alice.'

'You're welcome.'

'I wasn't … never mind.'

'Owen, you are one of the most intelligent people I've ever met. If you truly didn't believe you could do this then you would have found a way to back out gracefully. This is just nerves.'

'I know.' Owen sighed. 'Do you know how to make them go away?'

'The same way you do most likely. Focus on what you know, talk clearly, and don't ramble.'

TWENTY-FOUR

'Wise words.'

Her phone rang. It was a South Island number she didn't recognise.

'Aren't you going to answer?'

As a rule she didn't answer calls from unknown numbers so she rejected the call and put her phone back down. 'I'm sure they'll leave a message if it's important.'

'What's going on with you? Solved our latest murder yet?'

'It's only been a day!'

'So you're stumped,' replied Owen.

'I'm closer than I was. I just need to work out who did it, why, and how.'

Owen laughed, then stood up. 'Thank you, Alice. Somehow you always make me feel better.'

'It's a gift, sometimes a curse.'

Owen laughed again and as he left Alice realised how fond she'd grown of him.

She felt like closing her eyes for a short nap, but fought the feeling. Afternoon naps were for old people. She needed her brain working, not resting.

She decided to go for a walk instead. Perhaps the atmosphere at Charlie's would provide some inspiration.

As she approached the crowded café, Alice realised that what she was really after was company. She stifled the irritating thought as she caught movement to her right. Tracey and a gentleman in a suit were having a heated conversation. At least, it looked heated from Tracey's point of view. The man wasn't doing much talking.

As Tracey gestured wildly, she spotted Alice and waved for her to come over.

'Alice, would you please tell this detective that this facility is home to more than sixty people and the entire retirement village cannot be treated as a crime scene.'

Up close Alice could see that the man was in his mid forties, with short brown hair and an expression that hovered between interested and exasperated. He looked familiar, although she found that was the case with most people these days.

'Ma'am, that wasn't what I was saying. You are?'

'Alice Atkinson.'

'Oh yes. I recall seeing your name in the report. I would like to speak with you shortly.'

Alice inclined her head. 'At your disposal, Detective …?'

'Wilson. I am in charge of the investigation into Sylvia Gregory's death.'

'Sylvia Gregory's murder,' Alice corrected.

Detective Wilson's mouth twitched. 'The two are usually linked.'

TWENTY-FIVE

Wellington, March 1994

Marion's face showed her barely contained excitement and for a moment Amanda wondered if she'd gone too far with her story.

'It's horrible,' Marion gasped, though her tone didn't match her words. 'Why would someone take your grandmother's watch?'

Amanda shrugged. 'What's worse is that Alice – Gran – told me not to bring it to school, but I wanted to show it off because it's like fifty years old.'

'Is it valuable?'

'To my gran it is. My grandfather gave it to her before he died so it has all these memories and stuff. Anyway, after lunch I checked my bag and it wasn't there. I asked at the office this morning, just in case it had fallen out and someone handed it in, but it wasn't in the lost property. And now I have to tell my gran and she'll call the police and send someone to jail if they stole it.'

Antiques and Assault

'But how do you know for sure someone took it? Like you said, it could have fallen out of your bag.'

Amanda stifled her irritation. She'd already gone over this with Marion. 'Because of the note, remember?'

'Oh yeah, the note.'

'Now I'm trusting you with this because you're my friend. Don't tell anyone. It's a secret.'

'Oh no, I promise I won't say a word.'

Amanda hoped that wasn't the case. One of the reasons she'd picked Marion was because she liked to talk.

'Okay, thanks. I have to use the bathroom.'

Amanda walked towards the toilets but stopped just inside the door and looked back. Marion had wasted no time. She was talking energetically to a group of girls, then quickly moved to another. In five minutes she'd made it halfway around the playground and Amanda had identified at least ten children from her class who had been told the story. No one seemed to react with anything other than astonishment and one or two boys mimicked the sound of a police car. Amanda checked her watch. Thirty minutes left of lunchtime. She couldn't spend it all hanging around the toilets.

She waited a minute more then walked towards the netball court where a group of girls from her team were practising chest passes and bounce passes.

'Can I join you?' Amanda asked.

'We've got even numbers,' one girl replied.

'Sure,' Jenny said. 'We can change the game.'

Amanda joined the circle and quickly figured out what the rules were.

'So I hear you're in big trouble at home?' The girl who spoke had barely said two words to Amanda the entire year. It looked

TWENTY-FIVE

like her plan was working better than she thought.

'Nah, it's all okay. I just found out that they have security cameras in the hallways here. As soon as lunchtime is over, I'm going to ask Mrs Ferris to see them. Then I can go to the cops, get my watch back, and my gran won't ever know it's missing.'

Out of the corner of her eye something rushed towards her. She ducked too late and the ball hit her hard on the side of the face.

'I'm so sorry,' said Jenny. 'Are you alright? It slipped out of my hands.'

Amanda blinked away tears and clutched her ear. She felt anger sweep through her and clenched a fist. That's when Alice's voice came to her. 'You're more likely to be wrong when you react than you are if you act.'

'You should go to the sick bay,' said Jenny. 'I'll take you. I'm so sorry.'

Amanda nodded slowly, trying to focus on Jenny's words. She didn't sound sorry. Then again Amanda couldn't hear very well out of her left ear so maybe she was imagining things.

She wiped her eyes and followed Jenny to the sick bay. The room was next to Mrs Ferris' office and consisted of a bed, a chair, and a cabinet. Amanda had never needed to visit it before and she wondered what would happen if more than two children were ever injured or sick.

Jenny left her sitting on the bed, promising to find an ice pack for her face, and apologising profusely.

Amanda lay down on the bed to wait. Then immediately got up again. She went to the door and cracked it open in time to see Jenny go into the office. Amanda slipped into the hallway and checked both directions before approaching the

Antiques and Assault

office door.

'We can't even afford computers for the students,' Mrs Ferris said. 'What makes you think we have security cameras, you silly girl?'

'Dunno, someone said there might be some and my grandmother's watch is missing so I thought I'd check.'

'Sorry, Jenny, no cameras here. Tell your mother I'll call her tonight.'

The door to the office opened and Jenny stepped into the hall. She pulled it closed then turned and stopped when she saw Amanda.

'I'm sorry,' Jenny said.

'You said that already.'

'No, I mean I'm sorry I put the note in your bag. But I didn't take any watch.'

'So you admit you put the phoney note from Helen in my bag.'

Jenny held up her hands, her eyes wide as she vigorously shook her head.

'No, no. I didn't write the note. Helen asked me to give it to you. We were in class when I remembered and when you took off for lunch I just shoved it into your bag. I know I should have told you, but I swear, I just put the note in the pocket of your bag. I didn't see a watch. If it's gone then it was nothing to do with me.'

Amanda studied Jenny's face and decided she was telling the truth. 'When did Helen give you the note?'

'I went to her house after school on Thursday and she asked me to give it you the next day.'

'How was she acting?'

'How do you mean?'

TWENTY-FIVE

'Did she seem normal?'

Jenny frowned. 'I suppose so. She was a bit quiet but she seemed okay. Why?'

Amanda ignored the question. 'What did she say when she gave you the note?'

'She made me swear I'd give it to you the next day. She kept saying it over and over that it needed to be the next day.'

'Did you ask her what was in the note?'

'No. I mean I wanted to know, but you don't mess around with Helen. If she doesn't want to tell you something, she won't.'

'You didn't look?' That's what Amanda would have done.

'No! She'd sealed it and I didn't want to rip the envelope in case she found out,' Jenny admitted sheepishly. 'But I swear, I didn't take anything from your bag. I didn't even see a watch.'

'It's okay, I believe you.'

'Thanks, phew. Sorry again.'

Jenny raced off leaving Amanda with more questions than answers and this strange feeling that she'd just been lied to. Or maybe she was just feeling overly suspicious of everyone at the moment.

From the other side of the half open office door she heard Mrs Ferris.

'I'm telling you there is one missing. Look at the invoice. I signed for four reams of paper, not five. Well, that's not my problem. You either need to find it or replace it. Good, you do that. And when you've finished investigating you can let me know how you're going to rectify this.'

Amanda drifted away from the door, losing interest in the conversation.

After lunch Miss Boland asked her to get some photocopying

done in the office. Mrs Ferris was behind her desk and when Amanda explained what she needed, Mrs Ferris told her to wait out the front while she used the photocopier. While she waited, Amanda examined the photos on the wall. They were old class pictures and Amanda amused herself for a while with the dated hairstyles and clothing of past students and teachers. When she reached the last picture she turned and caught sight of a big bag crammed under the desk. Curious, she moved closer just as Mrs Ferris appeared and thrust a stack of paper at her.

'Thanks,' Amanda mumbled.

As she walked back to the classroom, Amanda realised she wanted to know what was in the bag. It probably had nothing to do with what was going on with her at school, but a big bag was a big bag. She spent the afternoon imagining what could be inside, then promptly forgot all about it when Alice picked her up and told her where they were going.

'That sounds like a bad idea,' Amanda said.

'Nonsense. It's long past time we had a word with Helen and now is as good a time as any. Especially in light of your successful endeavours today.'

'All I found out is that Helen wrote the note.'

'Yes. Now we know the who, we need to find out why.'

'Because she's a—'

'Undoubtedly,' Alice said. 'But there's more than that. Getting the police involved, planting her bracelet at our house – That's not only raising the bar considerably, it seems beyond the capability of a common twelve year old.'

'I could do it.'

'You, my dear, are anything but common. It suggests to me that there might be an older influence involved.'

TWENTY-FIVE

It was funny. On Saturday when they were driving to Helen's house, Amanda had been nervous. Today she was annoyed. She'd been willing to make up with Helen if it would make school more bearable, but not if she was being made fun of. She couldn't help feeling like this was all a big joke to Helen.

They pulled up outside the house and Alice turned to Amanda.

'Are you ready?'

'Do I have a choice?'

TWENTY-SIX

Wellington, August 2021

'You'll have to excuse me, Detective,' Alice said.

She nodded to Detective Wilson and walked over to the apartment next to Sylvia Gregory's. Moments earlier she'd seen a hand appear at the window and beckon to her.

The door opened before she could knock, and she slipped inside. 'Patricia?'

'Thank goodness. I didn't want to talk to that dreadful policeman again.'

Alice smiled and shut the door behind her. 'He's not that bad.'

Patricia De Burgh was shorter and thinner than Alice – a remarkable achievement given Alice's tiny size. Her nervous energy and the way she kept pushing her glasses up on her nose reminded Alice of a man she'd worked with in Hawaii once. Although his nervousness had been due to a drug addiction. Alice doubted the same applied to the woman in her mid-seventies. Alice hadn't often spoken to Patricia since she

TWENTY-SIX

moved in about eight months ago, but she was delighted to take the opportunity now.

'He asked me all sorts of personal questions,' Patricia said.

She pointed to a chair which Alice took as an invitation to sit down. Patricia sat opposite, her knees jiggling up and down and her fingers twisting together.

'Is everything alright?' asked Alice.

'What? Yes of course, maybe, no, I don't think so. There was a woman murdered a few metres away from me.'

'Of course. That must be disconcerting.'

'Disconcerting! Unnerving, disturbing, unsettling …'

Alice nodded. 'Yes, I can imagine so.'

'I met her once, twice. Here and there.'

'What did you think of her?'

Patricia seemed surprised by the question. 'Friendly, pleasant, sociable.'

Alice looked around the room and spied something on the chest of drawers in the corner.

'Patricia, do you play Scrabble by any chance?'

Patricia glanced at the game box and smiled. 'Yes, it's a very calming game.'

'Oh?'

'Creating words from letters forces me to slow down and focus.'

'You say you met Sylvia twice.'

'Yes,' Patricia replied. 'I introduced myself when she arrived, of course. She was here for tea only yesterday. Liked my angel.'

'Excuse me?'

Patricia pointed behind Alice. She twisted in her seat and saw three floating shelves on the far wall, and in the centre of the middle shelf was a figurine of an angel.

Alice quelled the flicker of excitement as she rose for a closer look. She reached out to pick the figurine up but Patricia stopped her.

'It's stuck to the shelf with Blu-Tack, so it won't fall over.'

'Do you know if there's a B scratched on the bottom?'

'Yes there is. How did you know that?'

'I've seen something similar recently.'

'How extraordinary. My late husband bought that for me at an auction many years ago. He said it was a one of a kind.'

'It's certainly rare.'

Alice studied the figure as well as she could without touching it. She'd only had a brief look at the one next door but they looked identical.

'You say Sylvia was interested in this?'

'Yes.' Patricia frowned. 'She wasn't excited about it though.'

'Excuse me?'

'Most people who see it are excited, like you are, but she seemed ... sad, unhappy, glum.'

'How strange.' Alice gave it one more look then turned to smile at Patricia. 'I suppose the police asked if you heard anything the morning Sylvia died.'

'All those questions. What time did I get up? Did I hear anything? Had I seen anybody lurking outside? You live here, the chances of someone lurking around Silvermoon without being noticed are virtually nil.'

'Agreed. Are you an early riser, Patricia?'

Patricia's eyes narrowed. 'That's just what he asked, the detective. Was she killed in the morning? Anyway, I wouldn't have heard anything. Whoever built these apartments made sure sound didn't carry from one place to the next. I thought it was one of the better things about living here. Some of these

TWENTY-SIX

places, it feels like the walls are made of paper..'

Alice thought carefully. 'What about Sylvia's granddaughter? Did you ever meet her?'

Patricia's expression soured. 'Met her? No. Heard her? Yes. What a nasty woman. If my grandchildren ever pulled themselves away from their screens long enough to talk to me like she did? My word. She was quite harsh towards poor Sylvia.'

'Where was this?'

'They were standing outside her apartment the day before she died. I wasn't trying to listen, but even when you're avoiding it you can't help hearing things. Do you know what I mean?'

Alice did, although she rarely tried not to listen.

'That girl told Sylvia to *do it* or be out on the street.'

'Do what?'

Patricia shrugged.

'Was this before or after she'd come to visit you?'

'After. She came that morning for tea.' Patricia sighed. 'Such a shame. When you get to this age you assume it'll be old age that gets you, not foul play.'

'Too true. If you'll excuse me, Patricia, I just remembered I was supposed to meet Vanessa at Charlie's five minutes ago.'

'Of course,' Patricia replied. At the door she stopped Alice with a hand on her arm. 'I hear you're a bit of a poker player. Let me know if you're ever interested in a *real* game.' She nodded towards the Scrabble box.

'You're on,' replied Alice.

No one was on guard outside Sylvia's apartment and Alice was tempted to nip in for another look around, but she didn't want to risk it without knowing where Tracey and the detective had gone. Instead she decided to follow her original plan and go to Charlie's to see what she could find out.

She was diverted a second time when, a few feet from the front door, she saw Vanessa step around the side of the main building and beckon to her. By the time she walked over, Vanessa had disappeared from view.

Alice rounded the corner and saw her standing at the edge of the carpark. 'What's going on?'

Vanessa's face was part triumphant, part excitement.

'I was watching Tracey like you said, but then she and that grumpy policeman went inside. While I was waiting for them I got to thinking about how no one showed up on the security cameras the night Sylvia died. That's when I remembered that while there's only one entrance for cars, there's more than one way for a pedestrian to get into Silvermoon.'

Vanessa led Alice to the back of the carpark. It was bordered by a tall hedge so thick it would have been extremely difficult for someone to push their way through it. Vanessa stopped at a spot that to Alice looked identical to the rest. Then Vanessa took a giant step to the left and Alice saw that what she'd thought solid was not. There was a slight break in the hedge hidden by an overlap. The gap was closed by a gate with a keypad lock.

'I'd forgotten this was here,' Alice said.

'At last! Something that's fallen out of the steel trap that's your brain.'

'Don't be too pleased, dear. I never had a need to use this entrance. I'm sure I would have remembered if the need arose.'

She peered through the gate at the short wide path that ran along the edge of Silvermoon for several metres before veering left. She remembered long ago requesting that this gate be put

TWENTY-SIX

in so as to always have a second exit.

'It links to the road behind us,' Vanessa said. 'I got the code from reception and checked it out.' She punched in the numbers and there was a click. She opened the gate and stepped through, with Alice following close behind. A few paces away Vanessa stopped and pointed at the ground by the hedge. Alice had to squint to see what they were looking at. There were faint shoe impressions in the dirt beneath the plants.

'So someone walked here.'

Vanessa shook her head. 'Look at the way they're facing. The toes are pointed towards the path. That means the person was standing here.'

'Waiting. You think this is how the killer got into Silvermoon.'

'It makes sense, doesn't it?'

'It does. Nice work.'

Vanessa grinned at the praise. Alice sighed as she led the way down the path towards the road. She needed to build up this girl's self-esteem. She should be satisfied with her own work without needing external validation.

The road they came out on was narrow with old houses set back from the road. It ran for about fifty metres in each direction before rounding corners.

Alice stood on the footpath slowly surveying the scene.

'What're you thinking?' asked Vanessa.

'The day before she died Sylvia visited her neighbour and discovered an identical valuable and rare statue to one she had in a box in her wardrobe. She then came to see us saying she was hiding from Helen and that Helen would be angry because she didn't want to do it anymore. She was then

Antiques and Assault

overheard by her neighbour having the same argument with her granddaughter. The next morning she's murdered.'

'So what didn't she want to do?'

'I have an idea but I need to make a phone call.'

They re-entered Silvermoon through the gate and Alice finally made it to Charlie's. It had quietened down a little. While Vanessa went to order their drinks, Alice sat at a table inside the front door. From there she could see Sylvia's apartment as well as the front of her own building. She checked both before pulling out her phone to make a call. A small blinking envelope reminded her she had a message to listen to.

She tried to recall how to retrieve it but couldn't remember the last time she'd had a message. When Vanessa sat down, Alice handed her the phone and she pressed the right buttons in a matter of seconds.

But could she lift a wallet from a closed handbag at a brisk walk? Alice thought.

'Hello, is that Alice's phone?' The woman's voice was vaguely familiar.

'Oh dear, I don't know if I've done this right. It's Ruth Hastings here, from Garden City. We talked about Sylvia?'

There was a pause as if Ruth was waiting for a response. Eventually she continued.

'I've been thinking about it since you rang. I think you should talk to Frannie Langston.' She slowly read out a phone number, then repeated it for good measure. 'She can tell you about Jacob's pride and joy.'

'Jacob's pride and joy,' Vanessa repeated when Alice relayed the message. 'What do you think that's all about?'

'I don't know,' Alice replied irritably. 'It could be anything.'

TWENTY-SIX

'Alright, no need to snap.'

'Don't tell me what to do.' Alice took a deep breath and admitted to herself what the actual issue was. 'Sorry Vanessa. I'm angry with myself for forgetting about the rear gate. It makes me wonder what else I've overlooked.'

'Alice. You can't beat yourself up for forgetting one thing.'

'It's a slippery slope.'

Vanessa was quiet for a while, no doubt thinking of a diplomatic way to agree with her.

'You've solved three murders at Silvermoon. No one else did that. I've seen a lot of things from you, Alice, but I never thought self-doubt would be one of them.'

Alice stared at her in astonishment. Their drinks were delivered to the table. Once they were alone again Alice spoke. 'I knew there was a reason I kept you around.'

'Is that all?'

'If you want effusive praise you're hanging around with the wrong old lady. Now, call Frannie Langston and see what she can tell us.'

'Oh yes, Ruth told me you might call,' Frannie said when she came on the line. 'Not sure how I can help you though …'

'Sylvia Gregory was murdered recently and we're trying to establish whether robbery might have been a motive.'

'Oh, I heard. It's horrible. Forgive me, but you don't sound like a police officer.'

'That's because I'm not. I live at the Silvermoon Retirement Village. I knew Sylvia and … well, this might sound callous, but I would prefer not to be murdered in my bed so I'm trying to figure out whether Sylvia was targeted or if there's still a threat to the rest of us.'

'Oh. Well, my dad died of natural causes if that's what you're asking.'

'Was your dad called Jacob? Ruth said I should ask you about "Jacob's pride and joy"?'

Frannie laughed. 'That's what he called his angel statue. He found it in a garage sale in the 1970s and always said it was the reason for his charmed life.'

Vanessa and Alice exchanged a look.

'Tell me, do you have the statue now? I mean was it in your father's possessions when he died?'

'I don't know, I think so.'

'Would you be able to check?'

'Why? Is it important?'

'It might be. Please.'

'Alright. His belongings are in boxes in the spare room. I haven't got around to sorting them yet. It'll take me a little while to go through them.'

'I'll wait.'

There was a clunk as Frannie placed her phone down.

'You think Jacob's statue is the one that's in Sylvia's wardrobe?' Vanessa said.

Alice nodded.

TWENTY-SEVEN

Wellington, March 1994

'I bet you're surprised to see me.'

Helen stood in the doorway, one hand on the door as if ready to jump back and slam it shut at the first sign of trouble. Amanda didn't know why. She'd never hurt Helen, despite definitely wanting to several times. There was a dark mark under Helen's left eye. She caught Amanda staring at it.

'What do you want?' She'd already asked that once.

'I came to say sorry.'

Helen looked confused and wary, but Amanda was surprised when she didn't look afraid. 'What for?'

'For us not getting along. I think it was partly my fault.'

'Is that all?'

'Who is it, Helen?' came a voice from inside the house.

'Just someone from school, Grandma,' Helen called back. 'Well? Is that all?'

'What else should I be sorry for?'

Helen snorted. 'Oh, I don't know. How about punching me

Antiques and Assault

in the face and stealing my bracelet?'

'I didn't …!' Amanda took a deep breath and continued in a more even tone. 'I didn't do either of those things, Helen.'

'Sure. I just got this by walking into a door.' Helen gestured to her face.

'I don't know how you got it, but it wasn't anything to do with me.'

'I know it was you. Now give me back my bracelet.'

'Honestly, it wasn't me. And if you say you saw me punch you in the face then you're a big fat liar.'

Helen's cheeks went patchy red. 'I'm not the liar. You might have worn a mask, but I know your smell.'

'My smell?' Amanda was bewildered.

'Yeah, that weird flowery smell your hair has.'

Amanda sniffed her hair. 'You mean shampoo? It's used to clean hair. You should try it sometime.'

'I use shampoo. It just doesn't stink like yours. And when you had me in the headlock, I could smell your hair.'

'So your attacker using the same shampoo as me was enough for you to send the cops to my house?'

'You stole my bracelet!'

Amanda thought of the bracelet tucked into her pocket. 'I did not steal your bracelet. Why would I?'

'You're jealous of me.'

'Of you? Not likely.'

'Then why did you say you liked all my stuff? I should call the cops. I bet you're here to steal more of my stuff.'

'I wouldn't touch your stuff if … if … if it was more valuable than the Cullinan.'

'The what?'

'Exactly. I only came here because my grandmother made

TWENTY-SEVEN

me.'

'Then sod off.'

'I will.'

Amanda took a step back then paused. 'Why aren't you at school?'

'None of your business.'

'You're not hurt and you don't look sick. How come you get to miss school?'

'I am sick.' Helen let out an unconvincing cough and Amanda laughed.

Helen looked furious. 'Go away!'

She slammed the door closed. Amanda jumped back to avoid her toes getting squished.

'How did it go?' Alice was outside, leaning against the car when Amanda returned to it.

'Really well.'

'Sarcasm is pointless, Amanda.'

Amanda sighed. 'It went badly.'

'Did you learn anything?'

She thought about it. 'Yes, I actually learnt a lot,' she grudgingly admitted.

Alice didn't say anything and Amanda ran through the meeting in her head.

'She knows it wasn't me,' she said.

'What makes you say that?'

'She wasn't afraid of me. I was supposed to have smacked her in the face, but she seemed mad, not scared.'

'People react to violence in different ways.'

Amanda leaned against the side of the car and sighed. 'I guess. There were some other things too. She said she never actually saw who hit her. She says she knew it was me because her attacker smelled like my shampoo. Only …'

'Yes?' prompted Alice.

'How would she even know how my hair smells? We don't sit that close to each other in class.'

'Perhaps in the school yard?'

Amanda shook her head. 'There's something else. She said I said I liked her stuff. I remember saying that once about her at school – but she wasn't there. Someone must have told her.'

'And?'

Amanda's head was filled with thoughts jostling for position. 'So someone else told her it was me?'

Alice smiled and Amanda realised she'd arrived at the conclusion several steps behind her grandmother.

'Why did you make me come and see Helen if you already knew?' Amanda said.

'Because you needed to figure it out yourself.'

'You still could have told me.'

'It won't stick in your head if you get it spoon fed to you.'

Amanda stifled her irritation, breathing deeply until it went away. 'Okay,' she finally said. 'So someone tricked Helen into thinking I'm out to get her. They attacked her, then made up the story about my shampoo. Then later on they stole my schoolbook and dropped it outside Helen's house so I'd be blamed for stealing her bracelet. But we already suspected all of that. How did this help?'

Alice opened the rear door of the car and gestured for her to get in.

'It confirmed some suspicions,' Alice said, 'which allows us to focus on the more likely suspect, and perhaps learn her motive.'

Amanda clicked her seatbelt and settled back in her seat.

TWENTY-SEVEN

'Jenny,' she said softly.
'Jenny,' Alice repeated.

TWENTY-EIGHT

Wellington, August 2021

They were on their way back to Alice's place. Frannie Langston had confirmed that she couldn't find her father's angel statue.

'So to summarise, we're thinking that Sylvia stole the angel figurine from the dead guy in Christchurch. When she moved here and saw an identical statue at Patricia's she told Helen about it. Helen wanted her to steal it, but she didn't want to. They argued and Helen killed her. Is that it? Case solved?'

Alice agreed that the story sounded plausible, but a nagging feeling at the back of her brain told her there was something she was missing. It seemed like extreme odds for Helen to have suddenly gone all psycho-killer on her beloved grandmother over the promise of a small fortune. Helen could just have stolen the statue herself.

As they entered the lobby, Alice saw the reception desk was empty again. The 'back in five minutes sign' was in place.

'Kerry isn't going to last long at this rate. Tell me, Vanessa,

TWENTY-EIGHT

when you worked on the desk were you away as frequently?'

'Are you kidding? Thanks to you I hardly spent more than half an hour at a time at the desk without getting called away for one thing or another.'

'It wasn't that bad.'

'Alice. The only difference between then and now is that I'm not wearing a uniform.'

Alice frowned and turned back to the empty desk. 'No, the difference between you and Kerry is she doesn't have me. So where is she?'

'She could be anywhere. She could be talking to Tracey.'

'Let's find out.'

'Why is it so important to find the receptionist?'

'I thought the official position was *concierge*.'

Alice led the way past the desk to the door marked Employees Only.

'That was *my* title. Kerry still has to earn it. And you didn't answer my question,' Vanessa said.

'Didn't I? How remiss of me.'

'Alice!'

'Surely, you don't need me to answer,' Alice replied. 'You already know why.'

Tracey wasn't in her office, so they retraced their steps. Alice stood studying the reception desk. Finally, she sighed and went to the elevator.

'Is that it? Wait! I get it. Change of routine.'

'Go on,' Alice said.

Vanessa jabbed the button excitedly before continuing. 'Before the murder Kerry was always at her desk. Since then, she's hardly ever been there. I remember you saying that changes in routine are a red flag. They make you stand out.'

'Excellent.'

'But it might have nothing to do with the murder. Maybe dead bodies just make her squeamish.' Vanessa punched in the code and held the front door of the apartment open for Alice.

'It's possible. Probable actually,' replied Alice. 'I'm frustrated. I feel like I have all the pieces of the puzzle, I just need to put them together. The explanation is so close.'

'Tea?'

'Eh? Oh, no thank you.'

'Something stronger?'

Alice shook her head. 'What I need … what I need is to get back into Sylvia's apartment.'

'How are you going to do that? I don't think the police are going to fall for the fake explosion sounds again.'

'No, a more direct approach is needed, I think. We're going to be invited in.'

Vanessa laughed. 'Sure, we'll just ask Sylvia Gregory's ghost if we can pop in for a cuppa.'

'We could.'

Vanessa clamped her mouth closed and stared at Alice.

'But I was thinking of a more conventional approach. Do you think you could find that detective fellow?'

'Sure, but why?'

'Because he's going to invite us inside.'

'How … No, you know what? Never mind. I'll track him down.'

While she waited for Vanessa, Alice went into her bedroom and sat on the edge of the bed. The double bed seemed tiny in the large bedroom. Vanessa had once asked her why she didn't get a king size or a super king size bed. She'd made

TWENTY-EIGHT

some flippant comment about not even knowing there was such a thing as a super king size bed. The truth was that some old habits refused to die. A smaller bed made it easier to roll out quickly in case a fast get away was needed. It was the same reason she always laid out her next day's clothes on the bed at night and put her shoes on the floor beside them. Her record from fast asleep to fully dressed and out through a window was two minutes. She doubted she was that fast now, but you never knew. Of course there was the other reason. The one she never admitted to anyone. The bigger the bed the more empty it felt.

She stared at the spot on the floor where she usually placed her shoes overnight. Then she swivelled her head and looked at the pillow. Beneath it was a night dress the style of which she'd sworn she'd never be caught dead in fifty years ago.

Abruptly she stood up, went back through the front door and to the elevator. She needed to get back into Sylvia's apartment. And soon.

As she reached the lobby, Vanessa came through the Employees Only door. Kerry was back behind her desk and she waved at Alice, who nodded at her.

'Right, Alice, the detective is in Tracey's office. He's agreed to talk to you.'

'Hello Mrs Atkinson,' Kerry said as Alice walked past.

'Good morning, Kerry. Oh Kerry, just out of curiosity. I came down earlier and noticed you were away from your desk.'

Kerry did an unconvincing attempt to look puzzled, then nodded. 'Oh yes, I was with Mrs De Burgh. She thought there was something wrong with her oven, but I managed to sort it for her.'

Antiques and Assault

'Well done dear.'

Tracey's office door was open and she was sitting behind her desk while the detective occupied one of the visitor chairs.

'Ms Atkinson. I understand you wish to speak with me,' Detective Wilson said.

'Yes, I thought I might be of assistance. I was in Sylvia's apartment the day before she died and I might be able to tell you if anything was missing.'

'You think robbery was the motive for her attack?' asked Wilson.

'It's *a* motivation, don't you think?'

Wilson studied her carefully before giving a nod. 'Alright. You will need to be accompanied of course, and you will not be allowed to touch or remove anything. Is that clear? I do not want my crime scene contaminated.'

Alice adopted an innocent look. 'Of course, Detective. I only want to help.'

She was glad the detective was facing her so he missed the look that crossed Tracey's face.

Tracey stayed behind in her office while the trio headed to Sylvia's apartment where Wilson unlocked the front door. Alice stepped inside and scanned the room, comparing it with the mental picture she'd taken on the previous visit. Immediately she noticed several small items missing.

'Is this exactly how it was before?' she asked.

'I'm supposed to be asking you that question.'

Alice smiled. 'Sorry, I meant is this exactly how the police found it? You haven't moved anything or taken anything for evidence?'

Wilson pursed his lips then said, 'Nothing has been removed – apart from the deceased.'

TWENTY-EIGHT

Vanessa made a choking sound.

'Everything alright?'

'Yes, just the casual way you said *deceased*, like she was a pile of clothes given to charity.'

'My apologies.'

Grateful for the Vanessa's distraction, Alice stepped further into the apartment. At least two, no, three things had been removed. All small, the sort of things that could easily fit into a suitcase.

She slipped into the bedroom while Vanessa and Detective Wilson were talking and went straight to the wardrobe. The box was open and she could immediately see the angel statue was missing.

'Ms Atkinson, I said you had to be supervised.'

Alice turned and smiled apologetically. 'Sorry, I was curious about the wardrobe space in these ground floor apartments. I never seem to have enough space in mine.'

Wilson frowned at her from the doorway. 'Can you tell if there is anything missing?'

'I can't be one hundred percent sure, but I believe there is a silver bowl missing from the coffee table.'

'And you can tell that from here in the bedroom?'

Game recognises game. Alice smiled again. 'I noticed it straight away but you were busy, so I thought I'd wait until you were free before mentioning it.'

Wilson glanced at Vanessa before turning back to Alice. 'Why do I get the impression you are withholding information, Ms Atkinson?'

'I have no idea. Perhaps it's the suspicious nature of a police officer?'

'Mmm. Can you describe the silver bowl?'

Antiques and Assault

'Certainly. Although I only got a look at it the one time so I'm not sure how much I'll recall.'

'Thank you.' He stepped back and gestured towards the front door.

Alice looked at the bed, then at Vanessa in the other room. Vanessa immediately yelped and clutched her leg. When Wilson whirled around, Alice swiftly went across to the head of the bed and lifted the pillow. She dropped it back quickly and peered under the bed. Straightening up, she felt her back tweak and grimaced in pain.

Alice hobbled to the door just as Vanessa miraculously recovered from her cramp.

'Are you alright, Ms Atkinson?' Wilson asked when he saw Alice.

'Oh, I'm fine,' Alice replied. 'Just a pulled muscle.'

'There must be something in the air,' Wilson said as he ushered both ladies out the front door. 'Is there anything else you would like to tell me, Ms Atkinson?'

Alice shook her head.

'No theories on who might have done this?'

'The murder or the theft?' asked Alice.

Wilson raised an eyebrow. 'You don't believe the two happened at the same time?'

Alice was almost certain they hadn't, but she couldn't say so without revealing that she'd been snooping around. 'I'm sure you know better than I, Detective.'

'Alice Atkinson. Any relation to Oliver Atkinson, the writer?'

'No,' replied Alice.

'He has the occasional *thought* as well.'

'I do like his books.'

'Mmm,' Wilson said. 'I'll send a sketch artist to your

TWENTY-EIGHT

apartment for the silver bowl.'

His phone rang and he held up a hand indicating they should wait while he answered it. He listened, spoke briefly, then hung up.

'Thank you for your assistance,' Wilson said to Alice. 'It appears this investigation has taken a turn towards resolution so I shouldn't need to bother you again.'

'Excellent. So you found the mover,' Alice replied.

Wilson was good, but not as good as her. His eyes twitched and a frown crossed his face.

'You know where to find me,' she said with a smile.

As they walked away Vanessa asked, 'Why did you do that? Let him know you knew about the mover?'

'Because that one is clever. And like most clever people he assumes he knows more than everyone else. People like that occasionally need reminding that's not always the case.'

TWENTY-NINE

Wellington, March 1994

'It's good to be back,' Mrs Kingston said.

She was standing on the school hall stage. The entire school was crammed inside for the assembly, with the teachers standing around the edges. Amanda sat at the end of a row halfway down. She'd deliberately chosen this spot so she could keep an eye on Jenny, who was seated two rows ahead.

Amanda had come to school that morning determined to confront her classmate. She'd expected Alice to talk her out of what she had in mind, but her grandmother had simply nodded and told her to keep a clear head. However, before she'd located her, everyone had been summoned to the hall.

Mrs Kingston looked better than she had in the hospital, but she still seemed a bit pale to Amanda.

'There has been a lot happening in the school over the last week or so,' Mrs Kingston continued. 'I know some of you are feeling nervous. I can assure you that our school is as safe as it's always been.' She smiled brightly, but Amanda thought it

TWENTY-NINE

looked forced.

As Mrs Kingston talked, Amanda looked around and realised that Mrs Ferris wasn't here. She frowned. Did Mrs Ferris usually come to assemblies? She'd never noticed. Alice wouldn't be happy to hear that.

She saw Jenny get up and creep to the end of her aisle. She spoke briefly to their teacher before leaving the hall through the back doors.

'As with all our assemblies we will start with the school song,' Mrs Kingston said. She gestured to one of the teachers who pressed play on a tape recorder. As the music began everyone got to their feet. Amanda took the opportunity to tell the closest teacher she needed to use the bathroom and slipped out of the hall.

She checked the toilets first, in case Jenny was there, but the closest girls' toilet was empty. From the hall came the sound of loud, off-key singing. Amanda hurried, not knowing how long the assembly would last for.

She raced to the classroom block and checked inside their classroom. No Jenny. Amanda walked down the central corridor quietly, her shoes squeaking on the grey linoleum, her weight on the balls of her feet, ready to react. Just as she approached the school office, the door swung open. Amanda ducked through the nearest door – a strong smell of disinfectant filled her nostrils and she realised she was in the janitor's cupboard. She held the door open a sliver.

Jenny was standing in the hallway with Mrs Ferris.

'Get back to the assembly before you're missed,' Mrs Ferris said.

She handed Jenny something and Jenny slipped it into her pocket and raced off towards the hall. Mrs Ferris watched her go before scurrying back into her office. Amanda paused to think for a moment, staying where she was, which turned out to be a good decision because a few seconds later Mrs Ferris remerged holding the large bag. Amanda had seen under Mrs Ferris' desk.

Mrs Ferris hefted the bag in the direction of the carpark. It looked heavy. Amanda followed. From the far side of the carpark, she watched Mrs Ferris lift the bag into the back seat of her car. She straightened up and looked directly at where Amanda was standing. Heart thumping in her ears, Amanda jerked her head back around the corner and ran towards the hall.

Just then the hall doors opened and students spilled out on their way back to class. Amanda slipped amongst them and fell into step with Marion.

'Where'd you go?' asked Marion.

'Toilet,' Amanda replied.

'Lucky. After the song Mrs Kingston went on and on about school spirit.' Marion's face brightened. 'But guess what? She said the police were going to be at school today. She said we should ignore them and do our school work like normal.'

Amanda looked sharply at her friend. 'Why are the police going to be here?'

Marion shrugged. 'She didn't say. Maybe someone tried to kill her again.'

'I don't think she'd be talking about it in assembly if that happened.'

Marion looked disappointed. At the classroom door Jenny cut in front of them and Amanda accidentally jostled her.

'Watch it, loser,' Jenny said.

Amanda mumbled an apology and made her way to her desk.

TWENTY-NINE

As the rest of the class got settled Amanda glanced down. She opened her clenched hand to see what she'd lifted from Jenny's pocket. She looked at Jenny, surprised. Why would Mrs Ferris have given her twenty dollars?

Miss Boland instructed them to solve the math problems on the board. Amanda raced through them in less than five minutes, then raised her hand and asked to be excused to use the bathroom.

The hall was empty as she walked towards the bathrooms. Then past them. Once through the outside doors, she raced across the carpark to Mrs Ferris' car. She crouched by the passenger door, shielded from the buildings. Her heart was thumping, and her hands shook. She took a deep breath, then another, and finally one more. Her hands steadied. She couldn't hear her heart anymore.

Mrs Ferris drove an ordinary-looking Mitsubishi station wagon. When Amanda saw her open it she'd used a key in the lock rather than one of those keychain buttons, so it probably didn't have an alarm. It still took longer than it should have for Amanda to pick the lock and she could almost hear Alice's voice telling her it wasn't good enough. The problem was she'd only ever practiced at home, and never with the pressure of being discovered.

Finally there was a click and the lock popped up. She peaked around the car. No one in sight.

Carefully she edged the car door open and grabbed the bag she'd seen Mrs Ferris stow earlier. It *was* heavy. Amanda unzipped the bag and pulled it open, expecting to find a computer or some other expensive-looking equipment.

Instead she found a pile of paper.

She picked up the page on top and saw it was an invoice for

a repair. So was the next one and the one below that. Amanda frowned. Why would Mrs Ferris be stealing invoices from the school office? It didn't make any sense. She flicked through the papers hoping to find some explanation, but they were all boring office type documents. She forced herself to look at them slowly. When she judged she'd been gone for as long as she could she zipped the bag up and closed the car door carefully, wincing at the loud click.

Standing straight up and looking casual, Amanda walked back across the carpark and through the double doors into the school. Before returning to class, she decided to go into the bathroom and wash her hands for appearances' sake. She walked over to the sink, turned on the tap and ran her hands under the faucet. She looked up into the mirror. And saw Jenny standing behind her.

Amanda whirled around, drops of water flying from her fingers.

'Where have you been?' asked Jenny.

'We're in the toilets, where do you think I've been?'

'You just came in. I saw you. Miss Boland wanted me to come and check on you because you were taking so long.'

Amanda realised this was her opportunity to confront Jenny.

She pulled the twenty-dollar note from her pocket and held it out. 'I think this is yours.'

Jenny shoved her hand into her own pocket and, finding nothing, realised what Amanda was saying. 'You thief.'

She snatched at the money but Amanda held it out of reach.

'First tell me why Mrs Ferris is paying you.'

'Give it here. I'll tell.'

'Like you told Helen I was jealous of her?'

Jenny shrugged and made another attempt to grab the

TWENTY-NINE

money. Amanda slapped her hand away.

'Give it!'

'Why did you tell Helen that I attacked her?'

For a moment Jenny looked confused, then she scowled. 'Because you did.' She sounded a hundred percent certain. 'Anyway, you got it wrong, like always. I didn't tell Helen you attacked her. She told me you did it.'

'Rubbish.'

'She was there, she would know.'

Amanda shook her head. 'It doesn't make sense. Why would she say that?'

'Because it's true.' She made another grab for the money and this time Amanda let her take it.

'I'm going to tell Miss Boland you stole this from me. Like you stole Helen's bracelet. You better look out.'

'Look out,' Amanda repeated. 'That's it! Mrs Ferris paid you to tell her if anyone left the assembly. You were her lookout.'

'Whatever. You're crazy.'

Amanda was thinking furiously, remembering earlier conversations she'd overheard and the papers she'd found in Mrs Ferris' car. Suddenly the one thing all those papers had in common became clear. The invoices were all from different businesses but the bank account for payment was the same.

'She's stealing from the school,' Amanda said softly to herself.

'I am not!'

'I need to tell Mrs Kingston.'

Jenny grabbed Amanda's top and pulled her in close. 'You're not telling on Aunt Glynis.'

Amanda grabbed Jenny's wrist and twisted it, breaking her grip and forcing her to bend over. Jenny yelped. Amanda kicked her in the shin and she fell to her knees.

Antiques and Assault

'Shut up,' Amanda said, 'and I'll let you go.' When Jenny didn't say anything else Amanda released her and stepped back.

Jenny gazed at Amanda in amazement, while gingerly rubbing her arm. 'How did you do that?'

'Practice.'

'That was awesome.'

'Er… thanks, I guess.'

Jenny's face turned angry. 'I'm going to tell Mrs Kingston you attacked me. You'll be expelled for sure.'

'No you're not.'

'How're you going to stop me?' Jenny was trying to sound brave but she took a step backwards.

'You're going to keep your mouth shut or I'll have to tell them how you're helping your Auntie Gly to steal from the school.'

Jenny's face went pale. 'You … I … you don't know anything for sure. Please don't. Mum would kill me.'

'Then you need to tell me everything. Starting with exactly what Helen told you about me.'

Jenny shuffled on the spot, glancing at the door. 'Okay fine. But I can't get in trouble again.'

'Spill it. Why does Helen hate me?'

Jenny snorted and shrugged. 'Helen doesn't hate you. You were a good excuse, that's all.'

THIRTY

Wellington, August 2021

'How did you know where I was?'

Alice adopted an enigmatic expression to avoid revealing that it was pure luck they'd found Helen so quickly. In fact Alice and Vanessa hadn't even been looking for her when they'd walked past the visitor carpark and spotted her car.

The back door was open and Helen was leaning in, her top half hidden from view. Which is why she hadn't seen them approaching until they were a few feet away.

'I don't have time to talk to you now, I have a lot of arrangements to make.'

'For your grandmother's funeral?' Alice asked. 'Or to dispose of the stolen items you just put into the back of your car.'

Helen was good. She immediately looked shocked, then indignant, drawing herself up to full height, which put her only just over Alice and still shorter than Vanessa.

'How dare you? I—'

"Yes, yes,' Alice said with a wave of her hand. 'How dare I, you're just a grieving granddaughter, etc, etc. I'm getting old so if we could skip the waffle and get on with it …'

Helen glared but Alice had been glared at by better so she wasn't fazed.

'A little tip for next time,' Alice said. 'Innocent people generally look confused rather than outraged when they're accused of something.'

'Are you a cop? No, don't answer that, of course you're not. Are you?' Helen asked Vanessa.

'No.'

Helen returned her attention to Alice. 'Are you going to call the cops?'

'Did you kill your grandmother?'

'No.'

'Even after she'd decided not to be part of your scheme anymore?'

Helen's expression turned wary. 'What do you think you know?'

'I know everything,' Alice replied. 'Apart from who killed Sylvia.'

'Oh sure you do,' Helen snorted. 'You don't know anything.' She turned around and fumbled the car keys from her pocket.

'You moved your grandmother into a retirement village. She would make friends with the residents, while identifying valuable antiques to target. She would tell you, and then you'd stage an incident. Suddenly Sylvia wouldn't "feel safe anymore" and would want to move, taking a couple of items that didn't belong to her. No one would suspect her. After all she was the victim. Her belongings were moved to the next retirement village, minus what had been stolen, which you would take and sell. How am I doing?'

THIRTY

Helen gaped with shock all over her face.

'Who beat up Sylvia?' Vanessa asked Alice. 'Was it Helen?'

Alice shook her head. 'No one assaulted her. It was an act. It's something Helen's been doing for a long time, isn't it? Pretending to be attacked to gain sympathy.'

'What?'

'Surely someone would have noticed.'

'No,' Alice said to Vanessa. 'All Sylvia needed to do was be too shaken up to be examined closely. And let's face it, no one suspected she was faking it, because who would do that?'

'You can't prove any of that.'

'Doesn't matter. What matters is that Sylvia told you she wasn't doing it anymore. Maybe she got tired of moving, maybe she developed a guilty conscience, maybe she just liked living here. But she was scared of how you'd react. And with good reason. You got angry. Especially when you found out there was a second angel statue in Patricia's apartment. The one you'd stolen from Frannie Langston's father was worth thousands, but a pair would be worth triple. You confronted Sylvia and hit her over the head. You probably didn't mean to kill her.'

'No! I mean, yes I was angry. We had a good thing going. But I would never have hurt her. She was my grandmother.'

Alice studied her face. There was something in Helen's tone that made Alice think she was telling the truth. If that was the case, she'd made a mistake somewhere.

'Besides, I knew she was getting old. I didn't want her to have to work forever. I already had a replacement lined up.'

'A replacement grandmother?' Vanessa said.

'Sure,' Helen said. 'It's just business. And I knew Sylvia was starting to lose her nerve.'

'She was your grandmother! And she's dead! Where's your compassion?' Alice put her hand on Vanessa's arm to restrain her.

'Well, obviously I'm sorry she's dead. But—'

'Helen, I'm going to take a look in the back of your car. I suggest you let me.' Alice made to move around Helen who stepped into her way.

'I don't think so.'

'Vanessa,' Alice said.

Vanessa grabbed Helen by the arm and twisted it up behind her back. She yelped in pain.

'Hurts, doesn't it?' Vanessa said grimly. 'I'm still new at it so I hope I don't twist too hard or I might accidentally break your arm.'

Helen instantly stopped struggling and stood still while Alice peered into the back seat. A familiar looking suitcase was tucked into the floorwell behind the passenger seat.

Alice pulled it out and laid it on the ground.

'I won't tell you the combination,' Helen said.

'Good, dear. That would be cheating.' Fifteen seconds later Alice opened the lid. 'It's always easier the second time.'

Three items were cushioned in foam. She recognised all of them from Sylvia's place.

'If these are stolen, why didn't you get rid of them before now?' asked Alice.

'You obviously know nothing about fencing stolen goods,' Helen replied. 'You can't just sell everything at once. People get suspicious.'

Alice decided that now was not the time for a lecture on fencing. 'Where's the angel?'

Helen scowled. 'I don't know. It wasn't where it was

THIRTY

supposed to be.'

'In the box in her wardrobe,' Alice nodded.

Helen opened and closed her mouth. 'Yeah. And that cop was hanging around so I couldn't do a better search. I thought I should get these other things out while I could.'

'Alice? Everything alright?' Alice turned and saw Owen striding towards them.

'Hi Owen. Why yes, everything is fine.'

'Are you sure? The way Vanessa is supporting that lady I thought there might be a medical emergency.'

Vanessa released her grip.

'Owen, this is Sylvia's granddaughter. She was suddenly overcome with grief and Vanessa was steadying her.'

'Oh, I see,' Owen said in a voice that plainly said he didn't. 'I'm very sorry for your loss. Vanessa, it's one o'clock. It's time to set up my computer for the video meeting.'

'Um I'm a bit busy right now, sorry Owen.'

'Don't be silly, dear. You made a promise to Owen and it's important we keep those,' Alice said.

Vanessa looked from Alice to Helen and back again. 'You sure you don't need me?'

'Of course. Helen and I have almost finished here anyway. Good luck with your speech, Owen.'

He flashed her a smile and straightened his tie like he was on camera already. 'Thank you, Alice. I'm as ready as I can be.'

'Come on then, I'll get you set up,' Vanessa said to him.

After they'd gone Alice turned to Helen. 'The police know some of Sylvia's things are missing. There are three things that can happen next. You could say nothing and hope that they don't look in your direction to locate the stolen stuff. You could hand them in to the police and say you moved them to ensure they were safe.'

'What's the third option?' Helen asked with a wary expression.

'Hand them in and tell the police Sylvia was a kleptomaniac and you were trying to protect her reputation.'

'Wait, that's it? You won't tell the police what we've been doing?'

'You didn't steal anything from Silvermoon, did you?'

Helen shook her head. 'Sylvia quit before we could line anything up here.'

'Then all I'm worried about is who murdered her. What you pulled off at the other retirement villages is of little interest to me.'

'Really?'

'Of course. But make a decision quickly. Detective Wilson is still poking around here and he might make up your mind for you.'

'You must want something.'

'Did you kill Sylvia?'

'No. And I had no motive. I called her from Auckland on the same morning she died and told her we would stop.'

'How did she react?'

'She sounded relieved. Happy. Said she was going to relax in bed for a while and go for a swim later.'

Alice didn't know what to believe, but she was tired of the conversation so she simply turned and walked away. As she walked she sent a text message to the number on Detective Wilson's business card. At the top of the steps to the foyer, she looked back to the carpark and saw Detective Wilson and a constable approaching Helen.

She smiled as she entered the building, but it slipped from

THIRTY

her face when she saw the reception desk was empty again. The Employees Only door opened and Tracey emerged.

'Alice, were you wanting something?'

'No, just wondering where Kerry is. She seldom seems to be at her desk these days.'

Tracey frowned and shook her head. 'I'm sure she hasn't gone far, but now you mention it she is absent quite a bit.'

'How did she come to work here?'

'I hired her. Recruitment is my responsibility as manager.'

Alice smiled. 'Of course, I was just wondering.'

'She came from a retirement village down south. She moved to Wellington a few months ago and had good references.'

'She's certainly friendly.'

'Yes, she is,' Tracey replied. 'I thought we'd struggle to replace Vanessa, but Kerry is proving adequate. Except for these recent disappearances.' Her smile brightened. 'Still, I recall Vanessa being away from her desk quite frequently.' She looked at Alice knowingly.

'Do you know where she is now?' asked Alice.

'Vanessa? No. Oh, Kerry? No, I don't know where she is either. Do you need her for something?'

Alice started to shake her head, then stopped. 'What was the name of the retirement village she worked at down south?'

Tracey looked startled at the abrupt change in topic. 'I don't recall. I could look it up. Why?'

Alice wasn't sure. The back of her neck prickled. 'You know me, Tracey, I like to know the people I see every day.'

'Alright,' Tracey replied, 'but you're not thinking of poaching this one, are you?'

'No,' Alice reassured her. 'One Vanessa is quite enough for me.'

'I'll be right back.'

As Alice waited, she idly observed the reception desk. Nothing seemed out of the ordinary, yet something nagged at Alice. She shook her head. Details were harder to recall than they used to be. Perhaps she wasn't up to this anymore. Maybe she couldn't protect her friends after all. A little shiver ran through her and she suddenly felt very tired.

'Don't be stupid!' she muttered. 'You're as sharp as ever. Now stop it or you'll have to kick your own butt.'

'Alice? Are you okay? Who are you talking to?'

Alice turned to see Tracey standing behind her.

'The most intelligent person in the room,' Alice said. 'Myself.'

'Er, right. I found the information you wanted. Kerry used to work for the Garden City Retirement Home in Christchurch.'

The name set off another alarm bell in Alice's mind. 'Thank you, Tracey.'

Alice had started towards the elevators and pressed the button. Suddenly what had been nagging her became clear. The little Lego figure was missing from Kerry's desk. The one she said went everywhere with her.

Alice abruptly turned and walked briskly out the front door.

THIRTY-ONE

Wellington, March 1994

Helen looked past the group of girls hanging off her every word and smirked at Amanda.

'I just don't know what I did to make her hate me so much.'

She'd been accompanied to class by Mrs Kingston just before lunch. The students were told they were not to ask Helen about her ordeal. It turned out they didn't need to. As soon as the lunch bell went, Helen had started talking to anyone and everyone who would listen. Once or twice, Amanda heard her name being mentioned.

Finally she couldn't stand it any longer. She walked up to the group. 'Helen, can I talk to you?'

All the girls gaped at her, like they expected Amanda to reach up and scratch Helen's eyes out.

'Don't do it,' one of them said. 'She's crazy.'

Helen tried to look afraid but couldn't quite pull it off. 'Unless you're here to say sorry then I have nothing to say to you,' she said haughtily.

'Please don't say anything. It'd just be a lie anyway,' Amanda said.

Everyone's heads turned to see how Helen would respond. Helen's face was bright red, without a trace of a bruise from her supposed assault.

Amanda sighed. 'Fine, we'll do it here, and everyone can hear about how you faked being attacked, planted your bracelet at my house to set me up, and how you're helping Jenny's aunt steal money from the school.'

Helen's face went pale and she looked around at the group. 'You did steal my bracelet,' she said.

'No one stole it, Helen. Did you even look for it properly? Everywhere? Like in your school bag?'

'It's not there.'

Amanda shrugged and fought the urge to tell Helen to check the small inside pocket of her backpack, where she'd slipped it before coming out to the playground.

They stared at each other until Helen looked away, glancing towards the carpark. When she looked back, her confident smirk had returned. Amanda followed her gaze and spotted Detective Graves and Constable Wilson climbing out of their car.

'They're probably here to arrest you,' Helen said.

'They're here to arrest someone,' Amanda muttered. 'Why don't we go find out?' she said more loudly.

She grabbed Helen by the arm and pulled her across the playground. At first Helen resisted, but Amanda dug her fingers in harder and Helen stopped struggling.

'Help!' Helen called when they got closer.

'What's going on?' Graves asked.

'She's crazy.'

THIRTY-ONE

Amanda let go of Helen's arm and the girl scuttled away to stand close to the policemen.

'Amanda?' asked Wilson.

She hesitated. She thought she knew what had happened, everything even if some of the pieces were a bit of guesswork. But she wasn't sure if the adults would believe her.

'We're here to discuss another matter,' Wilson said, 'perhaps we could come back and talk to you?'

'Stop treating her like a kid,' Graves said with a scowl. 'She's a delinquent.'

Helen was braver now she was standing between the two police officers. 'She's making up lies about me.'

'Oh, I don't think so.'

Relief flooded through Amanda as Alice walked up to the group.

'Mrs Strong, what are you doing here?' asked Graves.

'I didn't want to miss the ending,' Alice replied. She smiled and suddenly Amanda felt like she could do anything.

'We don't have time for this. We have an appointment to see Mrs Kingston.'

Graves made the mistake of trying to push past Alice. Amanda didn't see exactly what happened, but Alice did something with her finger and thumb and Detective Graves dropped to his knees with a yelp.

'Oh, I am sorry,' Alice said with a concerned look.

'That's assault,' he gasped.

'I know but don't worry, I won't press charges. Now let's all go to see Mrs Kingston. Oh and Constable Wilson, I trust you have your notepad and pencil. I have a feeling you'll need to take lots of notes.'

Amanda snuck a look at Helen and saw a mix of fear and

confusion.

Mrs Ferris' eyes widened at the sight of everyone trooping into the school office. She stammered something about Mrs Kingston being very busy, then looked at her watch and declared it was time for lunch.

'I think you might be interested in hearing this,' Alice said, as she stepped in front of the exit.

'Oh no, this looks like important principal business. You won't need me.'

Amanda thought she sounded bitter and Constable Wilson must have picked it up as well.

'Please join us,' he said firmly.

Reluctantly Mrs Ferris accompanied them into Mrs Kingston's office.

'Goodness,' Mrs Kingston said. 'I wasn't expecting such a crowd. I'm afraid I don't have enough seats for everyone.'

'Quite alright,' Alice said. 'I have a feeling some of us won't be staying long. Amanda?'

All eyes turned to Amanda and her mouth went dry. She licked her lips and looked at Alice who gave her a tiny nod, as if to say, you know everything you need to, now get on with it.

'Look here, this is police business,' Graves said. 'A crime has been committed. We don't have time to hear about your school yard disagreements.'

'Perhaps we should hear her out,' said Wilson.

Before Graves could offer any further protests, Amanda began.

'There were two separate events that happened at school in the last week. The first was Mrs Kingston being poisoned, and the second was an attack on Helen. Which the police thought

THIRTY-ONE

I did.'

'I told you,' Graves said, 'we're here about Mrs Kingston's assault. We don't have time to discuss a squabble between school girls.'

Far from being put off, Grave's tone and words made Amanda more determined.

'But that's just it, they were both the same thing.'

Everyone was staring at her, and she noticed not everyone was surprised.

THIRTY-TWO

Wellington, August 2021

'What on Earth are you doing here?' Alice asked Kerry.

Kerry smiled. 'I was checking on Patricia. She did have a murder right next door. I wanted to make sure she was alright.'

Alice nodded like she had been intending to do the same thing, which she completely hadn't. 'Where is she?'

Kerry's eyes flicked briefly towards the bedroom. 'She's having a lie down. The poor dear was feeling overwhelmed by it all. We should leave her to rest.'

'Yes, I'm sure you're right.'

Alice stepped back to let Kerry out through the door, then quickly slipped past her and into the apartment.

'Hey—'

'I'll just poke my head in and ask if she needs anything.'

'No! She's asleep.'

Kerry made the mistake of grabbing Alice's arm and pulling. Alice reached across and gripped Kerry's thumb, twisting it. Kerry yelped and dropped her handbag, falling to her knees

THIRTY-TWO

when Alice dragged her arm downwards.

She released Kerry and took two steps back, waiting to see what would happen next. Kerry just stared in disbelief.

'I wouldn't feel too bad about it, dear. You're not the first or last person to underestimate me.'

When it was apparent Kerry wasn't going to leap to her feet and rush towards her, Alice took another step back, putting a chair between them. Then she walked over to the bedroom door and pushed it open. The curtains were pulled and the overhead lights off, but enough sunlight pushed its way around the edges of the curtains to highlight someone lying in the bed.

'Patricia?' Alice called out softly.

There was no response. Alice looked back at Kerry to see that she hadn't moved then moved quickly across to the bed.

'Patricia?' she said, gently shaking her by the shoulder.

For a moment she thought the woman was dead, but when she looked carefully she could see Patricia's shoulder rising and falling. Next to the bed was a half cup of coffee. Alice picked it up and sniffed it.

A noise behind her made her whirl around. Unfortunately, she was still holding the cup and the contents splattered the bed. Swearing under her breath, Alice hurried to the door. Kerry was gone. From where she was standing Alice also saw where the angel statue had stood on the shelf there was now a splodge of Blu-Tack and an empty space.

Alice raced to the apartment door. Kerry was hurrying towards Charlie's. She set off after her but it only took three steps to realise she was never going to catch up.

Just then Vanessa rounded the corner of the main building.

'Vanessa! Stop Kerry!'

Vanessa immediately changed direction. Kerry broke into

Antiques and Assault

a sprint and raced past the café entrance. Vanessa caught her by the shoulder at the edge of the carpark. Kerry spun and smacked Vanessa in the face with her handbag. Vanessa stumbled and let go. Kerry turned to run again and Vanessa kicked at her knee, sending Kerry sprawling. She scrambled up and backed into a parked car, her hands held up in front of her.

'Kerry,' Alice called, shuffling towards them as fast as she could. 'It's over.'

'Nothing is over,' Kerry replied. 'You've got no idea what's going on.'

Alice took a breath. Despite the short distance from Patricia's apartment to the carpark, she felt a little winded.

'And that's assault. I'm calling the cops,' Kerry said to Vanessa.

'No need, the *cops* are already here.'

Alice cursed how easily the detective had snuck behind her. She really was losing her edge.

'Detective Wilson, just in time. Allow me to introduce you to our receptionist, Kerry Porterfield. She wishes to lay a complaint,' Alice said.

'Oh … no need for that. It was just a misunderstanding.'

'Was drugging Patricia and stealing her Bartholdi statue a misunderstanding as well?' asked Alice.

Kerry went pale and clutched her handbag to her chest.

Amateur, Alice thought.

THIRTY-THREE

Wellington, March 1994

'No one's going to listen to a twelve-year-old girl,' Mrs Ferris said.

'Waste of time,' Graves agreed.

'Go on, Amanda,' said Wilson.

Amanda took a deep breath. 'There was no attack on Helen. She made it up so she could point the finger at me. I thought it was because she didn't like me, but according to Jenny it was just because I was the new kid. I only started here a few months ago so it was easiest to fake a feud with me.'

'Why?' asked Wilson.

'They needed a distraction. They wanted everyone looking at me and Helen so no one would be looking at Mrs Ferris.'

'And what was happening with Mrs Ferris?' Wilson said.

'This is ridiculous,' Mrs Ferris said with a scowl. Amanda noticed she was licking her lips though. She was nervous.

'She was stealing from the school.'

'That's absurd!'

Antiques and Assault

'In the back seat of her car is a bag full of papers. Some are invoices, all for different places and things, but all with the same bank account number on them. I think Mrs Kingston got suspicious, so Mrs Ferris made her sick to keep her away from school for a few days so Mrs Ferris could dispose of the evidence.'

'That's ridiculous. Why would I wait until Frances was back at school before I, as you suggest, got rid of the evidence.'

Amanda shrugged. 'I don't know.'

'Tomorrow,' Mrs Kingston said. 'I was supposed to come back to school tomorrow, but I was feeling so much better I came back a day early.'

All eyes turned to Mrs Ferris.

'This is ludicrous,' she said. 'I didn't steal anything. I've always been very happy working here. Why would I jeopardise my career?'

'I did think something was up with you,' Mrs Kingston said to Mrs Ferris. 'The day I got sick was the same day I was scheduled to meet with a forensic accountant to go over the school finances. I came back from the bathroom and found a cup of tea on my desk. You said you asked one of the students to bring it for me.'

'Jenny is Mrs Ferris' niece,' Amanda went on. 'Mrs Ferris paid her twenty dollars to cause a distraction. But Jenny didn't want to get in trouble at school, so she convinced Helen to do it for ten dollars.'

'It was risky. The police could have seen through it.' Graves said.

'But you didn't,' Amanda replied.

'Besides, according to Jenny that wasn't the plan. Helen was supposed to say I stole her bracelet, but she decided that

THIRTY-THREE

wasn't exciting enough. So she'd made up the assault thing. She'd done it before, at her old school. Alice, my grandmother, talked to her old teacher and they thought she'd made it up to get the boy in trouble, but they weren't sure, and then Helen's mother took her out of school so the whole thing went away.'

Helen had been sitting quietly in the corner of the room. Now she burst into tears. 'I didn't mean to do it, it was Jenny's idea. She was my friend, I was just helping her out.'

Amanda felt a tiny bit sorry for her. Then she remembered she'd been visited by the police twice because of Helen, and the feeling went away.

'So there was no assault? No theft? The whole thing was fake?' asked Graves.

'That's what I just—'

'That's right, Detective, although I must ask you not to humour my granddaughter by pretending you hadn't suspected that all along.'

'Eh? Oh, well yes, things certainly hadn't been adding up. In fact I was heading over to talk to the Gregory's after finishing here.'

Amanda opened her mouth to protest but closed it again when she saw the warning look from Alice.

'Why did you let him take all the credit?' she grumbled as they walked to the carpark where their car and driver were waiting. Mrs Kingston had agreed to give her the rest of the day off school.

'It pays not to be memorable dear. Detective Graves believes he did it all on his own, and next time you meet him, if you ever do, he won't remember how clever you are.'

'So he'll underestimate me,' Amanda finished.

'Precisely.'

'But—'

'Mrs Strong?'

They turned to see Constable Wilson hurrying to catch up.

'Yes, Constable?'

'If I'd been in charge, I would have handled the investigation differently. Detective Graves can be …'

'An idiot?'

Wilson nodded with a faint smile. 'He's under pressure to take medical retirement. Solving this case would have got the brass off his back.'

He plucked at a thread on his uniform, then looked at Amanda before turning back to Alice. 'I hope we don't meet again.' He turned and headed back into the office.

'What did that mean?' asked Amanda.

'I believe it was a warning, and an acknowledgement.'

'What does that mean?' she asked again.

'It means that Constable Wilson is quite a bit smarter than his colleague. He'll go far. Remember his name, Amanda, it would pay to heed his message.'

'What about you?'

Alice grinned.

THIRTY-FOUR

Wellington, August 2021

'Before moving to Wellington, you worked at the Garden City Retirement Home in Christchurch. Coincidentally that's one of the retirement homes where Sylvia Gregory also lived before coming here. While there you heard about the attack on Sylvia. Then she moved out. I think you both turning up here was probably a coincidence. But when you heard she'd been attacked here, you began to think there was something more to it. Sylvia recognised you and when you confronted her she told you about the scam she and her granddaughter had going.'

'What scam?' asked Detective Wilson.

'Sylvia would move into a retirement village, befriend some of the residents and identify any valuables worth stealing. She would then fake being attacked and move out of her residence because she "didn't feel safe" living there anymore. Her loving granddaughter Helen would help her move, and they'd take a couple of extra items with them. Their last score was a rare

Bartholdi statue of an angel. What they didn't realise at the time was that the angel was one of a pair. Then, Sylvia moves in next door to Patricia, of all places, and what did she find when she popped in to introduce herself? A second angel statue proudly on display. But Sylvia had had enough. She didn't want to move again, so she told Helen she was done. Kerry saw an opportunity. She broke into Sylvia's apartment to steal the angel, and I think you'll find Patricia's angel in her handbag.'

Kerry tried to hide the bag behind her back, but Vanessa snatched it out of her hands.

'Oi!'

Vanessa handed the bag to Alice who opened it. Inside, carefully wrapped in a Silvermoon branded cloth napkin, was a Bartholdi angel statue.

She showed Detective Wilson. 'The statues as a pair are worth upwards of fifty thousand.'

'Miss, did you steal this statue?'

'I.. I …'

'Did she kill Sylvia Gregory as well?'

'Yes,' Vanessa said.

'No!' Kerry replied.

'Ms Atkinson?'

'I thought so, but …'

'What about the moving man?' asked Wilson.

'An inept thief. Even his employer described him as lazy and opportunistic. I think he probably pickpocketed Tracey's key-card, but when he realised it didn't open any of the apartment doors he made up some story about finding it. That's what he did, wasn't it detective?'

Wilson nodded. 'He said he found it, put it in his pocket and

THIRTY-FOUR

forgot about it.'

'But he had seen some valuable things when he'd moved Sylvia's possessions, so he snuck back into Silvermoon in the early hours of the morning.'

'But he didn't steal anything.'

Alice shrugged. 'Like I said, lazy and inept. He couldn't get into the apartment, so he left again.'

'So who killed Sylvia Gregory?' asked Vanessa.

'I can explain better in Sylvia's apartment'

'Fine.' Wilson handcuffed Kerry's hands behind her back before marching them all over to the apartment. He unlocked the door and they went inside. 'Well?'

'We're missing someone. Before we start, can I suggest you make a phone call?' Alice explained what she had in mind and he nodded.

He made the call and less than ten minutes later Helen walked through the front door holding a Charlie's takeaway cup. She suddenly looked alarmed at seeing Vanessa and Alice waiting for her, but smiled brightly at Detective Wilson.

'I wasn't expecting a welcoming committee. Detective, you said you were releasing my grandmother's apartment. I thought I'd come and tidy up a bit.'

'With a suitcase,' Wilson said with raised eyebrows.

Helen looked at Alice, then down at her suitcase. She didn't reply.

'Sylvia's body was found in her living room, fully dressed, just before seven in the morning. I know lots of people that like getting an early start on the day so the time isn't as important. But she told me she liked to lie in bed with a cup of tea and rarely got up before seven-thirty. In fact, on the day she died her alarm was set for seven-thirty but not turned on. So why was she up and dressed so early?'

Everyone looked at her blankly, except for Helen and Vanessa.

'She was waiting for someone,' Vanessa said.

'Not just anyone. Forgive me, Detective, but when I was in the apartment earlier I noticed something in the bedroom.'

Alice went there now, and lifted the pillow off the bed, revealing a neatly folded nightgown.

'So she was tidy,' Wilson said. 'I don't see … oh.'

Alice looked to Vanessa for explanation.

'She wasn't in a hurry. She got dressed like normal and folded her pyjamas under her pillow. She was relaxed.'

Alice nodded. 'Helen said she phoned Sylvia from Auckland and talked to her the morning before she was killed. But I think she was closer than that. I think she told Sylvia that she would come by and take her out for breakfast early to celebrate the end of Sylvia's life of crime. So Sylvia was up and dressed early, excited about her retirement. However, when Helen arrived they argued and she hit Sylvia over the head.'

'Why didn't she take anything with her?' Vanessa asked.

'No need. As Sylvia's heir everything went to her anyway. She just needed to be patient.'

Detective Wilson took Helen by the arm. 'Ms Gregory, do you have anything to say?'

Helen's face was transformed. As it contorted with anger, for a moment Alice thought she was going to launch herself across the room. Alice was a touch disappointed when her anger disappeared and Helen's shoulders slumped.

'Lawyer,' she muttered.

THIRTY-FIVE

Wellington, August 2021

'Helen Gregory has made a full confession and we have a list of previous residences where we can return the items still in her possession,' Detective Wilson said.

'Wonderful,' Alice replied.

They were in the rose garden, making the most of the pale sunlight struggling to heat the afternoon.

'Were you ever in the force, Ms Atkinson?'

Alice shook her head.

'You have a knack for it.'

'No need for insults, young man.'

'My colleague tells me this isn't the first time you've helped in an investigation at Silvermoon.'

'If by *helped* you mean *solved* for you, then yes she's correct.'

Wilson stood up and offered his hand. 'You remind me of someone I met early in my days with the police. She was a wily character as well.'

Alice smiled.

'How's your granddaughter?'

'Conquering the world.'

Wilson nodded goodbye and left her there alone.

Alice found herself thinking that Silvermoon was turning into a bit of a problem. She'd built it to give herself a safe, quiet place to live out her days. Yes, that had proven a mistake as her brain had threatened to turn into the same sort of mush the nurse said she should be eating for breakfast, until several murders made the place more exciting. Now her friends were thinking of moving, so maybe it was time for her to move on too. Although she claimed she didn't need anyone, she no longer entirely believed it was true.

'I've got something to show you.'

Vanessa crossed to the bench and sat down beside Alice. She passed over the electronic tablet she was holding.

'What's this?'

'Owen's speech. I recorded it.'

Alice tried to pass the tablet back. 'I'm sure it was a wonderful speech, dear. Perhaps later.'

'You really should listen to it, Alice. He talks about Silvermoon.'

'I thought his speech was about scams.'

'Just watch.'

Vanessa pressed play and Owen popped onto the screen. His voice came loudly through the speakers. Vanessa stood up and left Alice to watch it alone.

'Hello everyone. I have been invited to speak with you today about scams. They can be a serious problem, particularly for people of my advanced age. Now, I'm sure we've all heard the saying "if it seems too good to be true then it is", and in my lifetime I have come to believe that that saying is exactly

THIRTY-FIVE

correct. With perhaps one exception to my mind, and that's the retirement village where I live. The Silvermoon Retirement Village does seem too good to be true, but it is in fact, even better than it purports to be. Uhh, I'm getting off track. Now, everything else that seems too good to be true definitely is …'

Alice sniffed.

Silly old man.

THE END

Author's Note

At one point Amanda says she wouldn't touch Helen's things if they were more valuable than the Cullinan. The Cullinan Diamond is the largest gem-quality rough diamond ever found (21.9 ounces or 9.75kgs).

Frederic Auguste Bartholdi was a French sculptor and painter who was best known for designing the Statue of Liberty. He may or may not have designed two small angel statues.

About the Author

You can connect with me on:
- https://www.rodneystrongauthor.com
- https://www.facebook.com/rodneystrongauthor

Subscribe to my newsletter:
- https://www.rodneystrongauthor.com

Also by Rodney Strong

Other books in the Silvermoon Retirement Village series

Poker Chips and Poison

Hip Flask and Hanging

Knitting Needles and Knives

Printed in Great Britain
by Amazon